PRESS DIONYSUS

2020

First published in 2021 by PRESS DIONYSUS LTD in the UK, 167, Portland Road, N15 4SZ, London.

www.pressdionysus.com

Paperback

ISBN: 978-1-913961-02-2

Pantelis

A trilogy on mental illness

Kazim Altan

PRESS DIONYSUS

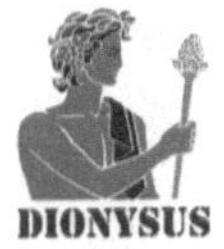

DIONYSUS

Press Dionysus •

ISBN- 978-1-913961-02-2

© 2020 Press Dionysus

First edition, November 2020, London

Cover design Semiha Deniz Akıncı

Cover photograph Tuncay Bilecen

Painting on the back cover Zübeyde Tuğsal

Press Dionysus LTD, 167, Portland Road, N15 4SZ,
London

• e-mail: info@pressdionysus.com

• web: www.pressdionysus.com

About the author

Kazım Altan was born in the village of Ayia Varvara in Cyprus. He completed his secondary education at Kurtuluş Lycee in Paphos and in September 1963, he came to London with the intention of studying law. By the end of that year, Cyprus was in turmoil and, inevitably, financial support, ceased.

He worked his way through further education, studied Sociology and Politics at MSc. level, and earned diplomas in Teaching English as a Second Language, Counselling, Educational Management, and ESOL Teacher Training. He enjoyed teaching, excelled in management and the quality of his work was noted and praised by The Office for Standards in Education and Training. He retired from his job as Assistant Director but felt retirement came too soon, so he joined Trinity College Examinations Board and worked as an English Language Examiner for several years.

Kazım enjoys writing and loves to combine it with performance. He has appeared in several shows at Arcola Community Theatre acting characters that he created. His theatre training culminated in a principal role in Ensemble 17, a musical play, written and directed by Jude Alderson, which showed at the Camden Fringe Festival in July 2017.

He has also written a play based on Pantelis which has some dancing in it. Sovronia dances to the tune of Adanalı, sung in Turkish and Greek.

In his mid-years, he spent a lot of his time setting

up and establishing a supplementary school for Turkish speaking children as well as a welfare association offering advice, counselling and support for the elderly. He did this alongside his full-time job. Not surprisingly, his children thought he was 'no fun' as a dad and that hurts even though it rings true! Kazım takes comfort in thinking he is a better grandad to two clever girls and two sensitive boys.

About Pantelis

In these multi-layered longish short stories in Pantelis, characters are fitted into a realistic world with life happening around them outside of their mental illnesses. As such it has a great impact on the reader. The characters are presented as whole human beings existing in the real world around us; they aren't 'just mad people'. Imagery is used effectively, bringing the work to life and allow readers to engulf themselves in the book by engaging their different senses; especially that of feeling and not just physically.

The book has the potential of building awareness around mental health in a creative, yet subjective way. This impacts on audience engagement and response as well as the reader.

Kemone S-G Brown

Some words of appreciation

My first book can easily be described as the product of the 'longest pregnancy in the history of writing' and the steepest learning curve I have ever had to climb. I am indebted to the writer, colleague and friend, Dursaliye Sahan, for her staunch encouragement and support; to Cathy Casimono Stephanides, for her patience in wading through my manuscripts and turning them into what they are in this book; to my friend, Baden Prince, for his valuable advice to accept edits with grace; to Richard Chamberlain for editing Patryk, to Kemone S-G Brown for proof reading the contents of this book; to my editor and publisher, Tuncay Bilecen, for taking the risk to publish my humble work and manage the whole printing and advertising process; to my sister, Zübeyde Tuğsal, who consented to have her very first painting decorate the cover page of this book, and last but not least, to my wife, Şengul, for her continuing encouragement and countless cups of tea and for tiptoeing around me for hours on end. I am also indebted to the many learners I have met, and people I worked with, who were inspiring to say the least.

In this book, I aimed to develop what I hope are universal characters who experience the joys and woes of life and display their frailties and humane qualities.

If you, my readers, feel any of them are like the people you know, then rest assured, each one is a product of my imagination brought to life before a laptop, sometimes, in the wee hours of the night. I hope you enjoy 'Pantelis: A Trilogy on Mental Illness'.

Kâzım Altan
November 2020

To my wife Şengül,
my daughters Halide and Cihan
and
their families...

'IN THIS WILD WORLD, THE LOVELIEST AND THE BEST HAS SIGHED, WENT TO SLEEP AND GONE TO REST.'

BLALOCK MISQUOTED

Pantelis

The old man wakes up early, a habit by now, a routine in his contracted life. It is a misty morning. He stretches out his aching body as far as it is possible for his 75 years, opens the window and breathes in the cold air of the Troodos Mountains. He is sprightly for his age, but he feels the weight of the years of toil in his muscles. The cold, fresh air hurts his lungs. It feels different to the air he is used to breathing in the backstreets of Stamford Hill, the congested streets of London, the dusty building sites where he worked. He tries to ignore the pain in his chest induced by the cold; he believes the cold air is good for him. He has spent most of his life in London, in need of and missing this sobering morning air, and he thinks he should be relishing it. He pounds his chest as he stretches as if to remind himself of this and looks up; there, he sees and feels the mass of the granite mountains.

'*My last day on the island,*' he reflects. Soon, he will be travelling to the airport and, once again, leave his homeland behind him. He loves this village, but he has things to do in London: rents to collect, and some work on a building site he has committed himself to.

His son had asked him to stay with him in the town so that he could drive him to the airport in the morning, but Pantelis had refused. He often refused such invitations lest his daughter-in-law feel he was imposing on them. When he did stay at Dimitri's house, Stella was welcoming, '*But you could never be sure with Stella,*' he thought, and this helped strengthen his resolve. Of course, it would have been easier to stay with them, to be driven to the airport in the morning - but he was glad he hadn't. Staying at the village was lonely but he valued his independence. He would drive his own car to the airport and leave it there for Dimitri to collect and drive back to the village, where it would be locked up in the newly built garage until Pantelis' next visit. '*Stella need not know of this arrangement,*' he thinks. He hopes that Dimitri will choose not to tell her.

At 75, he still welcomes the offer of the occasional full day's work, keeping in touch with contractors who call him up when they need walls built and plastered, fences erected. He is friendly with the directors of a Turkish Cypriot firm, and they often ask him to help out. He is glad for the offers, feeling useful, relishing the joy of being able to earn money at his age, feeling proud that his labour is still preferred over that of younger, stronger men, delighted that they like the quality of his work, the speed at which he continues to work, starting on time, finishing at 4 pm, never failing to complete the work scheduled for the day, convinced it keeps him fit.

'Pantelis, we have a small job in Central London. Are you able to help us out?' Kemal would ask him hopefully, mobile phone stuck to his ear. Pantelis would ponder a bit, holding back, delaying his response, believing it would not do to let Kemal know he is always available; he resents being taken for granted, and so his reply conveys hesitance, indifference.

'I have one or two things to do tomorrow. When did you want it done?'

'I like Pantelis. He is a knowledgeable man and very honest, hard-working! I learnt a lot from him when we worked together,' Kemal often made this comment in Pantelis' presence, and standard though it was, it never failed to please Pantelis. It heightened his self-esteem that he was seen as a good teacher and appreciated by his apprentice, who was proud of the way he had shaped him. Kemal had progressed in the business, was doing 'quality work,' and his clientele was growing. Pantelis had never been tempted to set himself up as an employer. He was content with doing a day's work and getting paid for it, preferably on the same day-although he accepted the weekly pay convention of the UK.

Kemal had introduced Pantelis to some of his friends and family. When Pantelis' wife, Gillianne, needed to get out of the house, he would visit a select few people, those he thought were more tolerant of the absurdities of mental illness. He never invited anyone back to his own house, and no one expected him to; they understood from what he told them that when Gillianne was well, their 'place' was 'spotlessly clean.' And Gillianne liked to paint, he'd tell them, "Apparently many of her paintings decorated the hall of what sounded like a three-bedroom 1930s terraced house with rectangular double bay windows, off Stamford Hill."

As a young girl, Gillianne had taught herself to play some music on an old out-of-tune piano. Sometimes, at the home of one of Kemal's relatives, she attempts to play these songs, producing the organ-like sounds heard at bingo halls or Butlins Holiday Camps, the notes of 1950s songs unsteady beneath her stumpy fingers, swollen by the heavy dose of tranquilisers she takes each day. Her good nature and spirited personality fill their host's room from the moment she arrives. She likes these people, trusts them, talks to them extensively about her illness, the things she does when unwell and how 'poor Pantelis' copes with it all.' She talks of her hallucinations, about the television speaking to her, her feelings of grandeur, her need to escape when she feels closed-in, and the irresistible urge to run away. The busy psychiatrists, compelled to give a label to mental illness, tell her she has schizophrenia. Gillianne wears the label defiantly, accepts that she is ill and in need of constant help and support, believes she suffers from schizophrenia and wants to talk about it-unusual for sufferers of mental illness.

More than anything else, Pantelis wants Gillianne to remain well. He knows that the strong tranquilisers help her to 'fit in' when she is on a 'high.' But when she is at her lowest ebb, he knows he must keep a close eye on her. If he notices early signs of 'change,' he locks her in before leaving for work. It's risky of course, and he worries about it in case a fire breaks out. He knows she could go out into the garden which is surrounded by an eight-foot-high wall. Climbing over it would be impossible. Leaving the house unlocked is too dangerous, so he advises her to go into the garden if necessary. And then he goes to work returning as soon as he can, careful to avoid his pay being docked, and takes her out for a drive in the car or for a walk in the park, gripping her hand tightly, holding her close lest she tries to run away. Next to him, Gillianne is large, well-built and her footsteps stomp on the ground heavily. She looks as if she is being dragged along. Gillianne complains that his pace is too fast for her.

She hates being a burden to Pantelis, hates it that he sticks with her still, supporting her. In the depths of her subconscious, she knows the love has gone, replaced by a sense of duty, responsibility that is Pantelis' nature. To her hosts, she recounts Pantelis' attempt to take her to Cyprus, to a 'calmer environment' where he hoped 'people would be kinder, less judgemental, being a smaller community, perhaps, more caring.' As she emphasizes the word calmer, she raises her eyebrows to suggest that the reverse is true.

'His plan didn't work,' she says, laughing uncontrollably, choking on her own tears. Her voice is high, metallic; she struggles to stop an almost frenzied urge to laugh.

'They regarded me as the mad Englishwoman chasing after a stray donkey in the nearby fields. The house was on the outskirts of Limassol, and I was as isolated as I was in London; my only companion was the poor donkey. I tried to protect it from the antics of the young children playing in the fields at the back of the house. Children can be very cruel, you know.'

Her statement is absolute, does not accept that children are likely to act without thinking when free from external influences. All this is said in one gasping breath, in a hurry, as if pronouncing her final words. Then, she stops; her smile freezes, her red-veined eyes stare blankly at a spot on the carpeted floor. In her mind's eye, she is re-living the life she lived on that island, in a lonely house, its backyard an open dry field. She sees the neighbours laughing at her as the children pull at her skirt, chanting names and abuse when she tries to protect the donkey. Her large figure twitches involuntarily as she reawakens to the present, relaxing her smile, looking around again but hardly making contact unless she decides to fix her gaze on one of her listeners. Her audience is silent, embarrassed for Gillianne, for Pantelis, for the thoughtless neighbours, for the cruelty of children.

Pantelis sits in a chair, his legs crossed and seemingly removed from everyone; he is detached and watchful, he smiles knowingly, murmuring the words kaimeni mou, my poor one, wishing that things would return to normal and give him some respite.

Pantelis takes a step forward pushing the image of Gillianne away, and buries it deep into his subconscious, although knowing it will resurface again, maybe within minutes, maybe much later. Now his thoughts are with his beloved mother, who is buried in this village. She died when she was 85, frail and somewhat confused. Pantelis had had to persuade her to leave the house in the village and be taken care of in a 'good nursing home' he found in Limassol. He hears Sofronia protesting in vain.

'*Ego, ti na kamo stin Lemesson re yie mou, enna me pareis sti Lemessianes*,'[1] she complains.

What, indeed, would an old lady, used to breathing the air of the mountains, do on the first floor of a care home, in a busy town where the traffic is constant and noisy and the people race furiously in all directions, seemingly without a minute to spare. There would be no one to talk to except the people who worked there, townspeople with airs and graces, distant, disinterested and in the margins of Sofronia's 80 odd years of life experience, talking down at her as if she were a child. There would be no one to visit her, at least no one she cared for, not like in the village where neighbours call; passers-by shout out greetings and misbehaving children annoy or delight the elders. He imagines Sofronia shaking her fist at the children as she walks towards them, trying to look threatening while the children run off and,

1 What would an old woman like me, do in Limasol that you are trying to send me there!

at a safe distance, respond by sticking their tongues out. But she was frail, and although still fiercely independent in spirit, she was unable to take care of herself. She needed caring, and Pantelis would not risk leaving her on her own.

Pantelis looks out the window, now fixing his gaze on the giant cactus, noticing that it is still in the early stages of fruit-bearing with bright yellow flowers at the tips of the emerging fruit. The cactus is called *papoutsosikia*, and it tumbles eight feet down the stone-walled garden; its branches will soon be lush with fruit, green turning golden, prickly but delicious. The wall from which it cascades is expertly built with granite stones of all shapes carefully placed, fitted in to resemble the structure of the cottage it surrounds. He recalls the toil that went into building it, the pride he had felt when he had finished it, thinking of it as a work of art, a master builder's creation.

In the summer months the fruit is ripe. During the early hours of the morning when the thorns are still subdued by the cool night air of the mountains, this fruit is picked with empty tin cans stuck on the end of a long wooden rod. He imagines Sofronia using one of these to reach into the thorny bush, trapping the fruit inside the can; twisting and breaking it off from the flat branches of the cactus. He sees her depositing it into a container filled with cold water from the nearby stream that hums its way down into the lowlands, sometimes rushing incessantly, at other times gently flowing. She repeats the action ritually until the bucket is full, the water spilling over to wet the parched ground. She leaves the fruit in the cold water so it remains chilled against the heat of the sun that will soon emerge from behind the granite hill that encloses the village within its shade. The sun will become more brilliantly intense as it moves across the sky, making the air hazy, lacing it with its brightness; visibility will be poor.

Later, but before the sun is out in full, Sofronia will take a knife and fork, cut both ends of the barrel-shaped fruit, slit the skin, push it back to avoid touching the many thorns decorating the peel—a skin hardened to protect the fruit from predators. Inside, there is a golden-coloured and surprisingly smooth sweet fruit which has a peach-like aroma. The large, flat, oval-shaped seeds in the centre are too numerous, with potential to cause an attack of appendicitis or severe constipation if too many were eaten. He sees Sofronia's weary face, concerned when her children had been eating too many cactus pears, and like when he was a child, he shudders when he hears her warning of this danger.

'*Panteli mou*, don't eat too many *papoutsosika* now. You know what happens when you do. Your tummy will hurt. You don't want that, do you? Come and give mummy a hug!'

Little Pantelis, sensing his mother's loving mood, drops the figs and runs into her arms, feels the softness of her breasts, her warmth and hears her soothing voice. She is dressed in the long-sleeved, long-skirted, high-collared clothing she always wears to protect her skin, and has on her head the inevitable black scarf-this is practically a uniform among the village women. Sofronia takes a few minutes to cuddle the boy, her fair-skinned mite, tiny and toddling, running around shirtless and shoeless. She feels comforted as the boy nests in her arms, pressing against her breasts, causing her nipples to rise, arousing her, the feeling confusing, pleasurable.

'*Ela 'dw yioudi mou, to yioudi mou, re yioudi mou.*'[2]

---

2 Oh my little boy, my son

'Come here my little boy, my little boy, come into my arms so we can keep each other warm. Do you know how much mummy loves you?' she sways from side to side as she tightens her arms around the boy. Pantelis is feeling suffocated, yet the feeling is also pleasurable. He tries to break away, opens his arms and gestures, his little arms embracing the air.

'This much,' he shouts.

'And how much do you love mummy?'

Pantelis opens his arms again to gesture the breadth of his love, this time without the accompanying words; he smiles, his little light brown eyes brightening but is also embarrassed so he casts his heavy lids down.

Sofronia protests, grimacing.

Pantelis stretches his arms as far out as he can and says, 'As much as the sea and the mountains!' He shouts it out and laughs uncontrollably.

'*It is funny that he should say*, "As much as the sea," thinks Sofronia. '*He has never been to the sea, never seen it, never known it.*' He had heard it was vast but had never been near it. As if sensing Sofronia's puzzlement, he omits the sea. He knows the mountains and gestures at them with enthusiasm, indicating their towering might, shouting the words out.

Now he sees Sofronia moving forward, picking up the boy, tickling him. It pleases her to hear his chuckles, straddling joy and pain, involuntarily turning into a scream. To the boy, she looks beautiful and loving behind the cruel mask—a face hardened by the years of toil, of grappling with poverty, of the leering advances of ill-intentioned men, the critical eyes of inquisitive women wrapped in black scarves, their feelings bordering on hatred and admiration, jealous of the attention she gets, secretly wishing some of it came their way. They gather at each other's houses to exchange news, to gossip, to condemn, the black scarves taken off for the short duration of a coffee break to reveal curly deep black hair of Venetian ancestry, skins hardened by the strong sun rays, tongues wagging.

The wealthier village folk serve the cactus fruit after meals or, in the hot summer months, as a cooling midday repast. Most nights when Pantelis went to bed, his tummy was filled with nothing but this fruit. On weekends, when the townsfolk came to 'take the fresh air,' Sofronia would peel and parcel some cactus-figs, half a dozen into each bag, and send Pantelis off to sell them on the side of the road that runs through the centre of the village, the town's 'High Street.'

'*Ela Panteli mou,*' he hears her calling him, sweetly. 'Take these up to the *kafenio* and sit there, by the side of the road. Make sure the figs are nicely displayed on the tray. People will see them and stop to buy some. They are a penny each, six Cyprus pennies or half a shilling a bag. These are pennies, and this is half a shilling.' She demonstrates, telling him to ask for six of the large copper pennies or one silver half-shilling coin for each bag of six figs.

'Don't let them bargain your price down,' she says firmly. 'They can afford that much I am sure.'

'In the meantime, I will prepare some treats for you… Now off you go. I hope you come back with your pockets full of money.'

The little boy weighed down by the heavy rush basket and the polished wooden tray with handles carved like vine leaves, walks down the cobblestone streets, the crescent-shaped handle of the basket too long for his tiny seven-year-old body. Relieved when he reaches the *kafenio*, he takes out two bags filled with cactus-figs and displays them prettily on the wooden tray. It was his grandfather who had hand-carved the tray; he is no longer alive, and Pantelis still misses him. Then the long wait begins. By midday, the townspeople start trickling through the winding, narrow streets and pass by the café. If he sells any figs, it is because the women in the cars notice him: a slight, undernourished figure wearing a faded shirt, ill-fitting, patched-up trousers and torn black plimsolls, his fair skin parched and freckled, sitting under the burning sun. The women wish to relieve him of the burden of waiting. They compare him to their own overweight children and feeling guilty for having the lion's share of good luck; they absolve themselves of any responsibility by buying him out.

Often, though, Panayi returns home with the basket still weighing him down. Sofronia consoles him:

'*Panteli mou*, you haven't sold any today. *Oi poutanes!* They didn't buy my boy's delicious figs.'

Embarrassed by the swear word, Pantelis chides his mum for being crude.

'Oh, Mum!'

'*Ela Panteli mou*, come and sit on my lap and give me a cuddle. I was only joking.'

Now he sees an image of his mother: thin, tall for a Cypriot woman, moving listlessly about in the garden. She fetches some wood, cleans the stove in the yard raking out the ashes and then shovels them into a tin container. Next, she places the iron cauldron on the stove. She bends down to light the fire, her eyes bulging from blowing hard on the dry sticks, all the time hoping it will light, impatient when it doesn't, when she must try again and again.

The cauldron serves for washing and cooking, but more often for washing. Ashes are saved and added to the hard water to soften it and to act as a cleaning agent. In autumn, the cauldron is used to prepare *trahana*[3], cracked wheat cooked in soured milk. The milk is kept in an earthenware container in the corner of their one-room cottage for several weeks, from the end of August until mid-October, and each day his mother tops the mixture with fresh milk from their own goat until the milk ferments into sour yoghurt. Pantelis remembers the taste of the yoghurt spread on freshly baked bread, his taste buds are awake now, and he salivates, craving for a bite right then.

When the yoghurt is sour, he remembers, it is stirred into the cracked wheat and cooked till the mixture comes to the boiling point. At that crucial moment, it is taken off the fire and let to set and cool. After this, it is time to knead the dough into balls the size of a small football. The women gather then, on the rooftops of the cottages, and using knives made of cane, they cut the dough into small strips, lay them in neat rows on a canopy also made of cane, where they will dry in the sun until they are hard. Here, too, the women talk of events past and present, tell stories, discuss weddings, exchange news of their young, attempt character assassinations and excite imaginations with news of improper liaisons, suspected love affairs.

Collecting and storing the dried *trahana* is a lonely business in comparison. It must be safely stored to be taken out in small portions to make soup during the treacherous but

____

3 Trahana / tarhana is a milk and wheat product cooked together, cut in small pieces and dried in the sun. It is used to make soup in winter months. Often fried 'hellim / hallumi' cheese is added to it to enrich the texture of the soup.

brief winter. Only around noon does winter's watery sun offer some respite. This is when the elderly women sit out on their patios, sheltering from the cold wind that whistles against stone walls as they sip coffee from miniature china cups, three fingers cupped over the dainty handles. They exchange news of their young, now departed to the suburbs of the fast-expanding towns or larger cities overseas, their needlework at rest on their laps.

September is when the goats 'turn' he remembers; in other words, they are 'on heat,' ready to mate; the kids will be born in the new year. When the female goats want to announce their 'turned' state and attract a mate, their bodies release pheromones or odorous chemicals. In his later years, Pantelis had looked it up in the dictionary, had searched the internet for it. He remembers the entry:

'Many mammals identify one another by means of pheromones. The males rely on pheromones to distinguish sexually receptive females from those still unreceptive.'

He remembers the males in the herds, excited by this odour, trotting majestically around the she-goats, smelling their tails, circling them and bleating gruffly. Meanwhile, the young shepherd boys try to steer the herds through the narrow roads of the village amidst the cries of women protesting that their trees, flowers, mulberry bushes are victims of the menacing goats who are indifferent to the vegetation. The 'boys' are focused only on the members of their harem.

The leaves of the mulberry trees are plucked and stored in the barns of larger houses or in the corners of the small cottages; this is the food of the silkworm. The worms feed hungrily on these leaves for several weeks before weaving their golden cocoons; their saliva spins the silk that encloses them for their long sleep and metamorphosis-which at the last stage means turning into butterflies, laying their eggs and dying. But to harvest the silk, to process it into thread, the silk cocoons must be taken to the bazaar before the butterflies can chew their way out, which breaks the thread. Remembering the smells—of the silkworm, its excrement, the hatching butterfly struggling to escape the cocoon— Pantelis feels sick, he feels the same nausea he felt as a child.

In his mind's eye, he watches the goats nibbling at anything they can reach as they rush down the hill: the young shoots of apple trees, of marrows, stretching out snake-like and bordered by brightly coloured pumpkins, the flowering hibiscus lining the roadside, the vine shoots camouflaging large bunches of blue-black grapes cascading from the pergolas, the precious mulberry bushes heavily pruned to ease the task of daily stripping of their leaves to feed the insatiable silkworms. Stretching their necks out, the goats assault the gardens along the road leading down to the valley. Singly or in twos, the goats are handed over to owners waiting at garden gates. The kinder, more understanding women stand at the side of their gardens and help the boys contain the herd, guiding the goats along the road, protecting the vegetation. Pantelis sees someone shriek as a goat strays towards her garden; she reaches out for the lush tips of the green vegetation and with one quick snap, releases these from their stem and chews on them, relishing the taste, defying the animated protests, the confusing anger of the two-legged beings. *'After all, what is more natural than a goat wanting to eat a juicy green shoot,'* Pantelis imagines them saying.

Sofronia was the first to notice that her goat was on heat.

'Panteli,' she would cry out, 'take the goat to the herd. She has turned.'

Pantelis remembers dragging the goat to the outskirts

of the village, the difficulty he had trying to hold her back when she made a dash for a tasty-looking morsel, raising herself on her hind legs to snap off a leaf or two from the mulberry trees along the street. In the distance, he hears the bells of other excitable goats as they roam the hills above the village, as they swoop down on the young sprouts and the slow-growing vegetation under the pine trees. The pervasive smell of pine is intoxicating. Villagers defy government rules, the forest by-laws, insisting on keeping goats for their agility on the steep hills, and refusing to acknowledge the damage the beasts can cause. They have no choice after all: life is harsh in the hillside villages, the productive land is restricted to a few strips that must be fenced in and protected from erosion by carefully built stone hedges. This is how they protect the apple trees, the tomato plants, the peppers and aubergines. The goats are essential to their livelihood, but at the same time, they pose a threat to forests; the contradiction seems insoluble.

Watching the goats on heat, the child Pantelis feels embarrassed; as a teenager, however, he becomes excited. Gamasha, the family's goat, joins the herd, hesitant and weary. The younger male goats approach her, some sniff her tail and move on, others butt her, rising on their hind legs, half-teasing, half-serious, chiming bells hanging from their long, graceful necks. One male goat, majestic and territorial, tirelessly circles each goat, checking out if any has 'turned.' The smell from Gamasha attracts him, and he charges towards her; drives away the young playful adolescent male kids. He is tall and powerful. Next to him, though not a small goat, Gamasha is diminutive. He circles her, sniffing, licking, bellowing. Gamasha plays hard-to-get-at first. She shoves, pushes, butts him playfully as he continues the ritual, always positioning himself for the moment when he might mount her. Now he rises, draws his hind legs closer, and with one big thrust, takes her–all the while standing tall and erect above Gamasha, who is crouched and shaking under his weight. He dismounts, breaks away, circles again, sniffing and licking his lips as he points his nose into the air, then looks again at Gamasha, wondering if he could try his luck again. But Gamasha moves on, disinterested.

Pantelis feels a warm rush of blood and is embarrassed at feeling aroused by such thoughts even after so many years.

'Oh to be young!' he mutters wistfully, his lips forming a sly smile.

He remembers that Gamasha produced much less milk during the weeks approaching autumn, and it was slightly tainted with the smell of pheromone. The milk is undrinkable, the smell overpowering, and there is not enough to make cheese every day. So it is used for the *trahana*, their precious winter food.

The gruel was tasty to Pantelis; '*It still* is delicious,' he thinks, his mouth watering at the thought. Westerners think it is a basic food with an 'acquired taste.' Pantelis is indignant at what he considers is a disguised insult.

'*It's just an unfamiliar food*,' he thinks, and as he recalls the offending words, he remembers the smell of cabbage lingering in the corridors of housing estates, the strong odour signalling lunch or dinner in UK houses. It was more so in his early days in London; now the city is multicultural, and it is the odour of kebabs or curry that he smells.

With his eyes still fixed on the cactus bush, he hears his mother calling him.

'Panteli, bring me the matches.'

'Where are they, Mama?'

'Next to the stove, where else!'

He watches himself picking up the box of matches, running to his mum; the verbal exchange is a ritual he often practices, asking a question so he can connect with her and elicit a response-no matter if it is an angry one.

As a child, Pantelis is small, skinny and fair. He has a sharp nose, thin lips, smallish light brown eyes with shapely eyebrows that are faint, lighter than the hair on his head. In his later years, he favours a pair of fawn-coloured corduroy trousers worn with a clean, white shirt. People who know him wonder whether it is just the one set of clothes he owns, washing and drying them overnight to wear the next day. He does not look like his brothers or mother, all of them dark-skinned–even darker in the summer months from the scorching rays of the Mediterranean sun. He goes bronze, then peels off in places, the light skin freckling.

Sofronia was from a poor family. Widowed at a young age, rumours surrounded her for the rest of her life. Some said she loved men too much. Others thought she was used and abused. But she survived the trauma of losing her husband and the shame of occasional illicit liaisons to focus on bringing up her boys. She seemed unblemished by the misfortunes, the 'mistakes' of her past. Pantelis thinks of her now: Always in her black dress and black stockings that she wore even in summer's high temperatures. Her scarf is tied over her forehead and under her hair at the back of her neck so that her long black curly hair cascades down. It reaches as far as her waist, and it swings from side to side as she moves around, busy with her work. Her voice is a commanding, deep contralto. Dark and tall and angry, she struggles for survival, working as a casual labourer when she is called to do so, gathering dried sticks from the hills, loading them on the back of her donkey to sell in the town, to houses sprinkled along the seashore, down in the lowlands, her clientele constant, loyal to her.

She loves Pantelis best because he is fair, and she believes he will bring the family good luck. Some say this intense love is perhaps 'transferred,' alluding to what they think might have been the result of a brief encounter. In later years when Pantelis is able to relieve her from her daily work, he sets her up as a *hanoumissa*, a *noikokyra*-a 'lady of the house.' He has enlarged the cottage and made it comfortable. Sofronia doesn't give 'a hoot' at what some people say. With fiery, almond-shaped eyes and a temper likened to lightning, she is respected and feared by the villagers. But she has needs and they know she will succumb, and she does from time to time, regretting it afterwards. The thought used to upset Pantelis when he was young. In his mature years, he thinks nothing of it, remembers his grandfather's philosophical line with awe, reminds himself of how the villagers were silent when he said coolly, redeeming Sofronia from the image of wantonness:

'An jini pou to exhoun theloun to, jini pou en to exhoun en tha to theloun?' 'If those who have it want it, why wouldn't those who don't?'

Pantelis continues to imagine her through the years. Her dark skin is darker still from the burning rays of the midday sun beating down on her as she cuts corn, picks fruit, bales hay or tends goats. She does whatever work rich folk ask her to do and is glad of it. Having tasted the warmth of genuine love, she rebuffs indecent advances; she now knows the difference.

Like all mountain folk, she has to be careful of the sun, shelter from it by covering her head with a black scarf and an old, tattered straw hat. The black scarf is a sign of mourning worn by almost every woman on the hills, committed to it from the day of the loss of a loved one. Sofronia had lost her husband within three years of their marriage to an accident on the granite hills of the Trodoos Mountains and has worn a black scarf ever since. Even so, the strong rays burn her skin, turning it a rich dark brown colour; to an observant eye, however, her skin is soft, silky, youthful.

'Up here, the air is cooler, fresher even though the mountains still roast under the same sun from dawn to sunset,' thinks Pantelis. Townsfolk came on weekends and at midday during the week, to escape the heat. *'It is easy to be 'tricked' by the cooler air, walking about unprotected from the sharp sunrays,'* thinks Pantelis, as he remembers how common it was for their exposed skin to turn red and painful by the afternoon of their visit.

'Panayia mou, ekaika, Blessed Mother, I'm burning,' they would exclaim, reaching too late for long-sleeved shirts to cover their burnt arms, taking up the sheets they had spread on the ground to picnic on and using them to cover their scorched legs.

'Englishmen also make this mistake,' he muses, as he visualises crowds descending on the seaside towns of southern England. Occasionally on hot days, when Gillianne was not well and he felt the need to keep her busy, he drove her to the seaside. Pantelis had a Volkswagen beetle, and he took good care of it, driving it with pride for many years. He drove Gillianne out of the city into rural England, believing that this would help her to get over her frequent cycles of hyperactivity. He dreaded the 'downtimes,' when depression set in and Gillianne stayed in bed all day crying; the normally spotlessly clean house becoming dusty, untidy, the threat of her running away, real. He thinks of the people at the seaside, walking about with their light skin carelessly exposed to the sun. By the evening, their whole body is in pain, scorched by the low sun rays of the northern hemisphere. '*The village people were in harmony with nature,*' he thinks, believing that his life experience had been painful but richer than that lived by the Western city dweller.

Gillianne had been a nurse. They met in the hospital when Pantelis was admitted with acute appendicitis. After the doctors removed the offending organ, he remained in hospital for a week.

'*Hospitals don't keep people for seven days anymore after a minor operation,*' he thinks. This happened in the early 1950s when Pantelis had travelled to the UK in search of work together with the first group of immigrants from Cyprus and other parts of the British Commonwealth.

'*Just how common was this wealth, which made it necessary for people to uproot themselves from their villages and towns to come to England in search of work?*' Pantelis wonders, embittered by the long separation from the land and people he wants to be with, those dearest to him, now departed.

Even then, he was a good bricklayer. He learnt his trade by working as an apprentice from the age of 11. His day's work was 'Worth a day and a half of any British worker,' he was told. This pleased Pantelis, who took great pride in whatever he did. He was reflective, interested in the arts; but it was not until late in his life, at age 70, that he earned a university degree in literature. He kept it quiet-why did anyone need to know? His late-life studies unleashed a new-or maybe even dormant-desire to research, to learn. The internet provided him with an inexhaustible source of knowledge.

His early days in London were lonely. He had arrived with just £10 in his pocket, barely enough to see him through a month. He found a bedsit with the help of some friends from Cyprus, and within a week, he had a job on a building site in central London. He lived modestly, spending little of his earnings.

'*A single room cost £1.50 in those days*,' he remembers.

Today he lets rooms himself, charging £85 and more a week. And although he has several houses, he refuses to pay taxes; he complains that he has no money to pay even as he collects his rents every week-at the same time, on the same day.

'I have to move about on the tip of my toes when I go to collect the rent,' he says to his friends. 'It is that dirty. But I don't care, as long as they pay the rent, that's all I care about. If they choose to live like pigs, what can I do about it?'

It is unusual for Pantelis to be dishonest. But he does not equate tax evasion with dishonesty. He feels his investment is hard-earned money on which he had already paid his taxes. He cannot see why he needs to pay any more of it to the treasury.

'I pretend I don't have any money,' he speaks these words insistently as if struggling to convince himself. 'When they send me a tax demand note, I make an appointment and go and see them. I tell them I have no money; I am unemployed. I plead with them to write it off. They agree.'

For anyone who has had any dealings with Her Majesty's tax inspectors, this does not add up—but somehow

Pantelis manages to get away with it. His wealth accumulates, and by the age of 40, he is almost a millionaire. And yet he continues to live frugally. He does not mind giving some of it to his adopted son.

'I have to see that Dimitri is ok. His wife is a bit difficult, I agree, but he needs to be in charge; earn enough to keep his family without having to beg from his in-laws,' he says to Gillianne, who agrees with him, although she is not convinced. Why does Stella deserve to live in such luxury when she herself scrapes and saves to manage the house on the small allowance she receives from Pantelis? The meagre allowance remains the same, only ceasing when she is too ill to manage; the last year of her life when she is strangely freed from her mental turmoil; a mystery to both.

Those early days in London were indeed difficult. He was cold most nights, and with no coal to burn, he had to wash and shave with cold water. His fair skin and light brown beard meant he could get away with shaving once a week without looking too unkempt. He used the same blade for many shaves. Liquid soap was diluted with water to make it last.

'I don't need much to live on,' he would say to his fellow builders—some of whom were also from Cyprus-while they ate together at lunchtime, whether out in the sun or under a makeshift shelter if it were raining or cold, around a fire lit using discarded pieces of wood on the building site. He hated the cold weather but was glad of the rain, a Cypriot gratitude. 'We need rain,' he would say gravely as if he were Einstein announcing the law of relativity. For lunch, Pantelis ate bread with onion. 'I was brought up on bread and onion,' he would pronounce amidst sneers and coarse laughter, seemingly enjoying this basic food.

'Go on Pantelis; treat yourself to an orange today. It will make a change!'

'Oh no… It may be a shock to your system if you do,' another would taunt.

Pantelis, undisturbed by the teasing, would eat his lunch quietly, rising to get back to work when his hour-long break was over.

His bricklaying was a work of art; every brick in place, just so! He knows this. He also knows that he is fast. Bricklayers worked with labourers who fetched and carried bricks and mortar. They still do. Every morning, the labouring folk argued about who they would be working with. Pantelis was difficult to 'feed.'

So, they argued among themselves, squabbling, feeling annoyed if they had to work with Pantelis.

'No, no, man! I am not working with Pantelis, today. I can't keep up with him, man! He needs two people to keep him going.'

All his life, Pantelis worked with pride, knowing that he was 'doing an honest day's work and a good job.'

He now gazes as far out as he can to the spot in the village square where he had, with a strong sense of urgency, built a small monument in memory of his mother. The love he had for her was like a dull, continuous pain close to his chest; the loss was difficult to bear. The memorial was a fountain with a tap and a basin beneath it providing water to passers-by, to goats and donkeys, dogs and stray cats. It was square-shaped, about 6 feet high, made of stone and the side where the tap and basin were placed was arched for effect. The inside was sealed to hold water. The inscription on the golden plate, 'In memory of Sofronia Stavrou Kashodis,

1907-1993', stands out baldly. This makes him feel proud, it makes him feel sad; passers-by say a prayer, murmuring, 'there, by the grace of God, go I,' fearing their own death, feeling vulnerable, and for a brief moment thinking of their worldly goods and chattels as worthless, meaningless.

'I missed her then,' he thinks, 'and I still do! It is strange how the pain never goes away. That feeling of loss, deeply entrenched in my unconscious, remains with me, day and night.'

'Closer than thinking, the dead woman hangs around my neck,

But never close enough to be touched or thanked even

For being all that remains in my world, smashed,'

Pantelis murmurs these lines to himself, misquoting Ted Hughes' war poem. In this final phase of his life, he feels embattled, vulnerable, sad. He feels his world crumbling around him, the decay starting with his mother's death.

His thoughts return to Gillianne. He misses her too but not in the same way. Perhaps this is not as strange as he first thinks; he is glad Gillianne is no longer suffering. He recalls their first meeting. She was warm and caring, jolly, unusually so, showing her gapped front teeth as she laughed loudly, breezing in and out of the ward, smiling, energetic. Beds were made, patients washed and sat in their chairs on the side of their beds, windows opened to air the ward, those needing personal care sensitively bed-bathed. 'How unlike today,' thought Pantelis, remembering the airless wards of the Northern Hospital where he sat watching Gillianne live through her last days.

In his youth, at this same hospital, Pantelis had felt a rush of blood in his veins whenever Gillianne came close to him. As this small, blonde young woman leaned over him, he felt his heart pounding, his flesh hardening, the sheets of the hospital bed rising slightly. Gillianne saw his excitement and lingered as if to tease him, first straightening his pillows, then lifting the sheets to check if he was healing well, whether the surgeon's cut needed re-dressing. When her hands touched Pantelis' naked thighs, he startled. Noticing his desire, Gillianne grinned; she continued to dawdle, caressing him with her eyes, teasing and exciting him, letting him know she knew what to do. When she drew the curtains around the bed to attend to him and leaned over him with her large breasts pressing against his slight body, her hands caressed more than the wound, perhaps accidentally, and he became excited beyond description. He had a tuft of light brown hair on his chest and hairy legs, signs of his youthful vigour.

The young woman was drawn to him. She felt her heart beat fast and her face turn scarlet. She stayed with him in the enclosed cubicle for as long as possible without raising suspicion in the ward.

On the third day, Pantelis grew bolder: when Gillianne came to dress the wound, he threw the sheets back to show her his hairy legs and chest. Gillianne, wide-eyed but jolly, teased the boy in him.

'Are you showing off your hairy legs and chest, Pantelis?'

Pantelis had blushed, but that same rush of blood erased the shyness of the mountain boy. Gillianne had come closer, leaning over him to straighten his pillows. He felt hot under the ill-fitting hospital pyjamas, especially with Gillianne's heavy breasts brushing against him. She was aroused too, her face flushed, her lips burning and expectant. She came closer, he breathed faster, and their lips met. In one quick flash, they kissed, Gillianne taking the lead. Her tongue explored the depths of his mouth, while his perfectly shaped teeth bit her lips gently. Her hand went down to his thighs, caressing his groin, feeling his hairy legs and landing on the small, hardened flesh. She guided his hands towards her breasts, but then she quickly pulled back.

'Now then young man, let's see how this wound is healing,' she spoke in a loud voice and used a perfunctory tone to let the other patients know that behind the curtains it was business as usual. Pantelis had come. A gash of semen landed on his chest. Smiling, she wiped it off with a wet flannel, redressed the scar, drew the curtains back and business-like, moved on to the next bed, leaving Pantelis wanting.

Throughout the rest of her shift, Gillianne made sure to stay away from Pantelis, afraid she might be caught and reprimanded for 'playing' with the patients; she was also worried that Pantelis might report her. She had acted on impulse. Nursing was her call. She did not want to lose her job. She had worked hard to get into nursing and was now in her second year of training. The ward kept her sane. During her hyperactive periods, she could find much to do and people would not notice; when she was low, she just seemed normal, since in the early stages of her illness her depressed state was very mild. She knew it would get worse. The disease was congenital. Her mother suffered from schizophrenia, and so did her two brothers. There was no escape from this illness. '*I must protect my job,*' she thought.

'*Anyway, I cannot get married and have children. This curse must end with me.*'

When she passed Pantelis' bed, she lowered her eyes.

At first, Pantelis felt rejected, but later, in a flash, he realised that she must be concerned about her job.

'What can I do?' he kept asking himself, worried that Gillianne was anxious. 'I should write her a note and assure her my feelings are genuine. But I cannot write in English!'

He decided that he would get help–by now, he had learnt a few words, phrases, and was able to communicate in pidgin English.

'Hey, Johnny,' he called out to his neighbour in the bed on his right, who had turned his back to him and was lying on his side, half asleep. All English men were Johnny to Pantelis.

'How do you say? I like you. Can you be my girlfriend?'

'You foreigners are all the same, sex-mad!' said Johnny, not so indulgently. 'What do you mean *How do you say*? You are saying it!'

'I mean, write, how do you write, I like you. Can you be my girl?'

'Oh, go away! I am in pain now. Ask me another time.'

Pantelis apologised and remained quiet for a little while before asking again.

'Go on tell me. It's important. Write it down for me. Here is a piece of paper.'

'Oh, all right,' said Johnny. Then, in his quick cockney tongue he asked, 'What's it worth?'

Pantelis looked blank. 'Worth?' he exclaimed.

'Yee, what do I get for it?'

'These Anglos, they don't understand the value of friendship,' thought Pantelis, 'everything is judged by money!' Pantelis liked money, of course, but only because he had a deep-seated fear of being poor. He had spent his childhood in poverty and wanted to make sure he would never want

for things again. But he would never say to a friend, "What's it worth?" for a little favour asked of him. He smiled wryly, and said, 'And what does a friend want?'

This was lost on the young Anglo-Saxon, a strapping six-footer, direct and brusque, who didn't give 'two hoots' for friendship with Pantelis.

Johnny sighed, shook his head, and finally gave into Pantelis.

Pantelis grabbed the note, thanking Johnny profusely. Then he folded it carefully and placed it under his pillow. He would give it to Gillianne the next time she came to dress his scar. He was sure she would make a good wife.

'*She would be a good company,*' he thought. '*Kind, caring and jolly. And she is sexy! She makes my heart pump fast every time I see her.*' He felt his heartbeat accelerating again. He lay back, he was hard, and as he caressed his groin, he felt the warm pre-cum on his soft skin. A slight touch and he was there. Feeling warm and satisfied, he dozed off and dreamt of his mother leaning over him, warning him.

'*Prosexse Panteli,*' she had said, getting closer to his face, whispering in his ear. 'Be careful of hasty decisions!'

Just then, a smooth, plumpish hand touched his thigh. He opened his eyes. It was Gillianne saying, 'Wake up. It is lunchtime.'

Pantelis smiled and felt his heart racing, his blood rushing through his veins, his body overheating. Embarrassed that he had come earlier and is unclean but aroused, he reached under his pillow for the note and discretely placed it in Gillianne's palm, closing her hand gently over the note. Gillianne understood, smiled, blushed and carried on serving his lunch, this time distant, avoiding physical contact.

'*More of this English food,*' thought Pantelis, missing his customary bread and raw onion.

He moves sideways now, stepping out of the PVC patio doors of his modernised cottage. His home was once just a one-room cottage with an outside loo, and he shared this room with his mother and two brothers. The garden was a yard with a shelter for the goat and the donkey they kept. A tiny part of it was fenced off to grow some tomatoes and vegetables. The goat had three kids each year, and these were fattened and sold at the village festival to supplement the family income. His father was dead or maybe just not with them. He never knew which. Whenever he asked, he sensed his mother's tall, slight figure tensing, the skin on her tanned, thin face tightening, dismissing the demand, brushing it away.

'Never mind your father. He is not here.'

Each time they had such an exchange, Sofronia's eyes gazed into the misty valley below the house and saw the fair-skinned, slim man holding her hand, taking her to bed in a room at the inn in the town centre, his arms enveloping her, his fingers caressing her lips. They had lain on the bed where he took her gently, lovingly; they both held tightly onto each other, filled with an unexplained desire to embrace endlessly. Then it was time to go—too soon for Sofronia who was starved for love. Fehim rose, dressed and went to work; Sofronia left after him, walking the opposite way lest she be recognised by a passer-by. They met this way every Saturday. Within weeks, Sofronia knew she was pregnant.

Fehim was captivated by this woman of the mountains. She was the woman in his dreams: dark, direct, wiry, but soft and loving too. They had met at the bazaar, the *pan-*

topolion, where everything anyone could produce, was sold. Vegetables, tomatoes, seasonal fruit, grape juice products like *soujoukon*, sausage-shaped sweets made of a string of almonds or walnuts, dipped in grape juice thickened in flour. The remainder of the batter was chopped in square shapes to turn *palouze into Kofterga*. The sweet *soujoukon* and squire pieces of *palouze* were dried in the sun and carefully preserved in earthenware pots to be sold in the autumn months; the chief customers were the folk who liked to drink *zivania*, the local firewater.

Some stalls were filled with milk products, such as *haloumi and anari*, and others sold the emblem of the island, precious olives. They were part of the staple diet, but the busy city housewives would buy them too, to offer as a delicacy with cocktails. There were vendors selling village breads, *tsoureki, flaounes, paximadi* and soda bread. A few sold trays of golden and mouth-watering syrupy, sweet cakes. In the corner of the bazaar stood the halva shop displaying all varieties—plain, with chocolate or with pistachio nuts, and pita bread to accompany it. On the windowsill that served as the counter stood the scales on which pieces of halva were weighed and wrapped in grease paper and served from the window. There were also a variety of handcrafted goods, embroidered table-cloths and doilies, which sat side by side with firewood.

The domed bazaar was overfilled with an array of colourful stalls-so many that a number spilled out onto the roads leading up to it. The bazaar had several entrances; Sofronia had a place at the entrance leading to the Turkish quarters of the town. She sat facing Fehim's halva shop.

Every Saturday morning, she was one of the first to arrive. She tied her donkey at the inn, gave it some hay, filled the tin container with water, and took her designated place to display her goods: wood for the fire, what she could spare of the family's *trahana, anari* and *haloumi*, some dried beans, *papoutsosika* depending of course on the season, a few ripe apples, some tomatoes. Perhaps a few cobs of corn or some Lefkara embroidery if she had managed to finish a piece.

Fehim watched her as she moved to and fro; setting up, emptying, displaying, straightening, heaping her various goods that she hoped would earn her some money to feed her children.

'*How beautiful,*' he thought, '*who is this vision?*' He tried to get closer to her. Any excuse: Did she need some help? Would she like a Turkish coffee? Was she comfortable? Would she like a chair he could spare from the shop instead of that stool she was sitting on? Was she hungry? Could he offer her a *kofte*, a *keftede*? He had just bought some. They were fresh and still warm and tasty!

Sofronia was slowly coaxed into his net, but knowingly, willingly; she was drawn to this smooth operator with light brown hair and green eyes that turned honey-coloured in strong sunlight. Their conversations reached a level of intimacy that encouraged Fehim to propose hiring a room at the inn, plotting a discrete meeting to make love. This was a small town. They needed to be cautious for the sake of Sofronia as much as Fehim. The innkeeper was a friend of his. They could have the end room closest to the entrance where Sofronia could slip in without anyone noticing, he'd suggested.

Burning with youthful desire and trusting this kind, handsome man, she agreed. She packed up her goods and piled them on the side of the road, covering them with the sacks she had brought them in.

'*No one will touch these*,' she thought, as she started walking towards the inn, hesitant, excited and longing to be loved. She entered the courtyard now just as she would for several months, slipping in through the door of the first room. At the far end of the room, next to the iron bed stood Fehim, holding two glasses of red wine. Sofronia advanced, taking two steps; then she stopped to think again. The image of her two sons and dead husband loomed largely, yet her desire for Fehim was greater. He came forward, offered her a glass of wine, and then held it to her lips as he encircled her from behind. She drank, he drank some more, and they embraced one another passionately.

Soon they were on the bed, making love, now gentle, now rough, lovemaking that heightened and calmed as their mood changed. Neither embarrassed nor ashamed but head over heels in love, Sofronia emerged undetected from the room and hurried to pick up the donkey, collect her goods and make her way to the village where her young awaited her. She felt Fehim at her side, with her, in her, enveloping her; she spoke to him as if he were by her side, holding her in his arms. Her short-lived marriage was an arranged one. She had felt much respect for her husband but no love. Fehim, she loved. And so, out of this intense but short-lived love, Pantelis was conceived. How could she tell Pantelis? But then, how could she not tell him in the face of his persistent questioning?

He stoops to avoid hitting the *anari* cheese hanging out to dry in a stocking on the washing line. Reproaching himself for forgetting to pack the cheeses, he grabs them, hurriedly stuffs them into a plastic bag, and then carefully places them into his suitcase.

Anari is Pantelis' favourite cheese. He uses it to complement the macaroni dishes he cooks for himself more and more these days. It is an easy dish and a wholesome, filling food. He loves the taste of *anari* with the macaroni, and disagrees with dieticians who warn him that it is fattening.

'Everything in moderation is good. One should never be over full, with food,' he thinks aloud, echoing the words from the Koran, 'fill your stomach with one-third food, one-third water and the remaining third leave empty for breath.' Perhaps, being a curious man, he had researched the command, had made it part of his own philosophy.

Almost involuntarily, he turns and goes back to the garden; he wants to remain in the past and is annoyed that his reverie has been disturbed. He remembers how years later he came across the Italian cheese called parmesan and thought how similar it was to *anari*. 'Nor,' he says, remembering how his Turkish friend refers to this cheese.

'*A small world*,' he thinks, amused by the clichéd expression that comes to his lips. 'The world was always big. We just got too clever and are now hell-bent on destroying it,' he says to himself, angrily at first and then indulgently as befits his 75 years. It is as if, like Prospero in 'The Tempest,' his mellowed self is signalling preparation to depart. He enjoys reading, often weighing up his own life experiences against those of the characters he encounters in novels and poems. He especially loves short stories and hopes one day to write a story about his beloved mum.

His thoughts return to the hard-working woman who grew up on the hillsides of the Troodos Mountains and had lived there close to a century; the depth of his feelings of loss intensifies merges with the loss he feels for the father he never met. More than anything else, he wishes he had known his father. But he could not insist. The piercing, angry eyes of his mother always warned him that this was a line that could not be crossed.

He did not learn about his father until he was a grown man, on one of his annual trips home to visit his mother. He loved these times, where he spent every day talking with her; or rather, she talking to him as he patiently listened. He was devoted to this tiny woman, more so now in the final phase of her life. He recorded everything she said, knowing there would be a day soon 'when her diminutive figure and large soul left the departure lounge for good, for God.' Pantelis smiles at his ingenuity, his way with words. He is proud he has mastered the language of his adopted country.

In the midst of one of these conversations, Sofronia lowered her eyes and apologised to Pantelis, revealing her weakness for this man she had so loved.

'He was a good '*Turkos*,' she said, 'not like the others.'

Although Pantelis was enraged, he did not want to hurt her. He let out a sigh and said simply:

'I wish you had told me earlier. I wanted to know him. It's too late now.'

Indeed, it was too late. Following the civil strife at the tail end of 1963, the Republic of Cyprus—which had been established only three years prior, in 1960—collapsed. Demarcation lines were drawn, and Turkish Cypriots were forced to live apart from the Greek Cypriots in enclaves, most suffering poverty and want. In 1974, during the attempt to overthrow the Greek Cypriot administration by EOKA B, and achieve unification with Greece, inter-communal fighting broke out once again. Fehim had left his halva shop and was trying to get home to take his family to a safer part of the town when a bullet went through his heart and ended his life. He was but 64.

'I didn't feel it as much as I felt the pain of parting with Sofronia,' he would have said, if he had been able to. He died instantly.

Tears run down Pantelis' cheeks now as he paces the garden, cursing those who manipulate difference to further their own power and control. He is even more unforgiving towards those who allow themselves to be taken in, those who assist the narrow-minded in drawing lines and artificial borders, taking precious lives.

Time is getting on. Pantelis tries to calm himself as he nears the edge of the garden, taking in the view below the stone wall: the winding cobblestoned roads, the lush green pines, the apple trees dressed as brides in pinkish-white outfits; old men ambling towards the kafenio, old women feeding chickens, younger women milking goats, children wiping their sleepy eyes as they look out of windows to check their mothers are still around to protect them. There are sheep bleating, sad to be separated from their young lambs; young men hurrying towards the village bus stop as a light wind whistles; cockerels, flamboyantly extending a single colourful wing that sweeps the ground, circling the hens; kid goats agilely jumping up on the barn roofs as protective mother goats try to coax them back with panic-stricken cries.

'*How ironic*,' he thinks: men, women, children and beasts all live together in harmony in this village; yet the harmony is not universal on this ill-fated island in the far eastern corner of the Mediterranean Sea-an island that for millennia has been subject to invasion and conquest by myriad foreign powers, Venetians, Lusignans, Ottoman Turks, and more.

Just then, the rising wind intensifies. Soon the angry

waves, set on a race towards the rocky beaches, will submerge the Rock of Aphrodite. Pantelis awakens from his daydreaming, walks back into the house, picks up his case and his car keys, turns off the electricity, walks out and locks the door. He looks down at the valley once more, takes a deep breath as if for the last time, and strides purposefully towards his car. The neighbour waves good-bye; he revs the engine and is gone.

He is late. 'I was dreaming far too long,' he thinks, chiding himself. He could miss the plane. They would not refund his money. He hates waste. He presses on the accelerator, racing down the narrow road bordered by cliffs. He feels his blood pressure rising as he rounds the sharp bends of the winding road. His foot slips off the accelerator; he panics and loses control. The car skids as it descends and hits the side of the mountain, head on. As it jolts and then stalls, Pantelis slams on the brakes. The car jumps sideways and tumbles over the cliff. It somersaults once and then again, hitting a rock jutting out of the sharp granite cliff. The car turns, and somersaults again, now sideways, once, and then again and again. With a mighty crash that echoes against the hills, it lands on its side, trapping Pantelis between its metal wings, now bent, broken, sharp-edged, treacherous. Yet it continues to descend and somersault. Pantelis is semi-conscious and tries to move his trapped arm, but his head hits the roof and then the side of the car as it turns and rolls until it finally reaches the valley. With one last jerk, it grinds to a halt. The sound of metal against rock echoing on the granite hills startles the villagers who bow their heads and make the sign of the cross. The village warden calls for help, the church bell strikes. Still semi-conscious, Pantelis sees his mother smiling, his beloved Gillianne in the middle of a tree-lined road beckoning him, the two women welcoming him to the world he always wondered about. He is pleased to see them standing happily together. Pantelis' face suddenly contorts into a grimace and he loses consciousness.

The stream rushes furiously down the valley, and then becomes subdued as if humming a lullaby for Pantelis, who has drawn his last breath on the mountains he so loved.

***

Gillianne

'They called me *the mad Englishwoman*', said Gillianne, referring to the time when they had lived in Limassol. In full flow, she jumped from one subject to another. She was about to embark on what was by now a familiar account of her mental state. She would talk about how she felt when she was ill. The various things she would do, the worry she involuntarily inflicted on others; she noted the denial of ill health by so many suffering from a mental illness, just as she did in the early stages. 'We refuse to take our medication. That's the biggest problem,' she said. Silence ensued.

Sonay spoke up, 'But they have so many side effects. Maybe that is why you didn't want to take them.' Sonay spoke, not with her authority as the pharmacist that she was, but to show her empathy and compassion for Gillianne. But Gillianne did not believe that Sonay was speaking honestly, and she remained silent. She thought she was just being kind to a sick older woman.

When she did respond, it was with undisguised self-depreciation.

'No, it's because I am mad; I am stark raving mad. I do not know how Pantelis puts up with me. He is truly kind. You are exceedingly kind, aren't you, Pantelis, and very good to me? I don't know what would have happened to me without you. I would probably be locked up in some mental institution and forgotten about. I don't know why you married me; why did you marry me, Pantelis?'

A smile broke out over Pantelis' face—a face that was usually neutral and devoid of expression. '*Kaimeni mou*,' he murmured under his breath, 'my poor suffering one.' He recalled the early days of their relationship, which had begun in a North London hospital. At the time he was barely nineteen and had been admitted with acute appendicitis. Gillianne was a young student nurse who seemed almost driven when she attended to her duties.

Her energy impressed Pantelis, who believed it showed dedication to her job. He understood well how a person might have an internal need to work hard and aim for perfectionism.

He was a bricklayer, and he built walls as fast as is humanly possible and as neatly as the most skilled craftsman. He measured windows and patio doors with precision, built strong and straight walls, and plastered them with a speed that surprised but also infuriated fellow builders because he set a standard they could not match.

As he gazed at the evenly laid bricks, he felt satisfied and happy with the outcome of his efforts. 'Pleasing to the eye,' he would say in later years when his English had become fluent.

Kemal often wondered about the reason for Pantelis' energy and determination, and what was behind the flat, expressionless look in his small brown eyes. Angry or happy, his expression was constant. Extreme emotions were a rarity with Pantelis.

'Where did you learn the trade, Pantelis?'

Pantelis relished this chance to reminisce, to look back at his life and reflect on his "rags to riches" story. Yet despite all the wealth he had gradually accumulated, Pantelis still chose to live modestly.

'Ah, Kemal… I come from a low-income family. There were days when we had nothing to eat. I went to work as a builder's mate at the age of nine and was taken on as his apprentice when I was eleven. He was a hard man. Sometimes I thought my back would break with the work he expected me to do.' He chuckled as he often did when embarrassed; he made light of his harsh upbringing, and his eyes gave nothing away.

'But he taught you well, I think.' With this remark, Kemal was praising Pantelis, but, in truth, he was also trying to encourage him to say more. Kemal, like his sister, Sonay, was very generous in his appraisals of people and was always ready to compliment them on things they did well, and note their good qualities.

Pantelis pursed his lips. He was not good at accepting compliments, and he sensed this might have been one. But the comment triggered memories of the builder, stocky, short and robust, with a round weather-beaten face. He thought of him putting on his overalls, mixing mortar, carrying it up the ladder, placing it on the scaffolding and beginning work that would continue non-stop until lunch break. From the very beginning, Pantelis had to keep up with him. He was no more than a small skinny boy, unused to hard labour. Vasos was demanding.

'Come on Pantelis, move. I have no bonding left. You know we must be quick with this material,' he said, gesturing at the nearly set bonding. Impatient and almost desperate, he urged Pantelis to quicken his pace.

'Maestro, it's hard to keep up with you.' Pantelis' voice

was full of pain, and his eyes silently pleaded to be understood as he tried harder to please. His back was hunched with the weight of the bricks or mortar he carried up the ladder.

'No excuses, Pantelis. I was younger than you when I started work.'

Vasos remembered how he had struggled to keep up with the builder he was apprenticed to. His growing muscles had ached at night, and the pain was still there when he woke up—he was so stiff that moving was a challenge. There were days when he felt he would never make it to the next, and here he was spurring on little Pantelis, treating him just as he had been treated. For an instant, he felt sorry for bullying the little mite.

Pantelis' muscles ached as he struggled to mix the bonding, place some in a bowl, crawl up the ladder to the makeshift scaffolding to hand it over to the Maestro. Within seconds—before Pantelis had hurried down the ladder—the plaster was laid on evenly. Arms akimbo, Vasos stood and watched Pantelis shovelling the remaining mud. He liked the boy and knew he was a hard worker. Then, worried that if he was too indulgent, Pantelis might slacken his pace, he bellowed, 'Not good enough, Pantelis! Not good enough! By the time you go down to fetch the remaining mud, it has set. It's a waste of material and my time. I am standing here waiting.' Then, almost as an after-thought, he would give Pantelis instructions.

'You should be preparing some new mud before the last one finishes. At this rate, we won't be able to build a goat's pen, never mind a house.'

'Yes,' thought Pantelis, *'it's easy for you to say, but I am just a boy and an under-nourished one at that.'* But he kept at it. He gritted his teeth, ignored the pain in his weak muscles and raced to keep up with the Maestro. Especially in winter months, when the occasional, northern wind from Siberia blew bitter cold, he shivered in his short khaki trousers and threadbare shirt. These days were hard to bear, and he almost wished Vasos was dead.

But with time, his muscles hardened and developed, the pain subsided, and he felt stronger. He was taller; his chest had expanded, his hands were rough with callouses. And he had become much faster at getting things done. This pleased the Maestro, and he began to talk to him about his life, his work and occasionally about the finer points of his trade, which he usually kept to himself.

'I have been doing this job for nineteen years,' he once said, but almost immediately he remembered his apprenticeship and added another six years.

'I mean twenty-five,' he said, 'and I am still learning.' Building materials change almost daily. You have to keep up with new things.'

Pantelis smiled to himself as he recalled his apprenticeship days. He often wondered what had become of Vasos when he left for London.

***

Coming slowly out of his reverie, Pantelis returned to Gillianne's question: Why had he married her? Shrugging his shoulders, he cited the same stock answer he always gave:

'It is as God wanted it to be.'

58

He seemed unaware that this sounded dutiful and hurtful to Gillianne. The thought that Pantelis stayed with her out of a sense of duty and not because he loved her or even that he cared for her, intensified Gillianne's feelings of insecurity. As Pantelis remarked that it was 'God's will' Gillianne felt the weight of this compelling fate. But Pantelis was deeply religious, and he truly believed that he had to accept and be content with whatever God willed. He certainly did not mean to hurt Gillianne, nor to make her feel indebted to him.

When Pantelis realised that Gillianne went through phases where her personality changed, he accepted this as his fate and as 'God's will.' He even thought, perhaps, he and Gillianne were brought together by providence so that he could take care of her when she became ill. He failed to hear the charitable tone in this philosophy that guided him through his life and dictated his relationships, not just with Gillianne, but everyone he knew.

***

Gillianne became clinically ill shortly after their marriage. Pantelis was a simple soul with limited knowledge of such things. He had fallen in love with Gillianne because he found her kind and warm. He also thought she was attractive, even sexy.

On that fatal morning, Gillianne woke up early and switched on the television. It must have been about 5:30 am. She sat in the dining room attached to the small kitchen at the back of the house, looking at the television screen, stunned, when Pantelis walked in. He was drying his face with a threadbare towel that looked as though it had passed its 'use by' date. He seemed refreshed, full of energy. He had shaved and showered the night before so he would be ready for work in the morning. From the kitchen, he called out to Gillianne, 'Tea, love? Gillianne? What's up?'

'Pantelis, Pantelis, look! They are talking about me. They are saying I stole a packet of biscuits from the supermarket! I never, I never did that!'

The TV presenter continued with the news item:

'Shoplifting is on the increase. The report says people steal because goods are displayed attractively in stores and invite those who cannot afford them to help themselves. It costs stores many thousands of pounds to keep this crime checked. Shoplifting is a euphemism for stealing. Store managers believe that the term makes the act of stealing somewhat more acceptable. The report recommends that signs in shops make it clear that "shoplifting is stealing" and those caught are thieves who will be prosecuted.'

'Pantelis, Pantelis, listen to this, they are saying they will prosecute me. Oh my god! Will they put me in prison? Who will look after you?'

Pantelis came into the room and listened to Gillianne, observing her closely: her face was flushed a bright scarlet, and her eyes were panic-stricken.

'What you talking about? She is not saying that! She says that Shoplifting is wrong. It is stealing. We know that, don't we?' These utterances disguised how alarmed he felt.

The presenter went on, 'Shoplifting is not done out of need. In our welfare society, poverty is a relative term. In this country, there are no poor families who need to steal to eat. Experts blame advertising for creating needs by over-promoting products. People who steal do so because they feel they lack something or other that they, too, should have.'

'You see, you see! Pantelis, she is saying I am a thief.'

'*Agapi mou*, they are not talking about you. They are talking about people who steal. You don't steal, do you?'

Gillianne stood up and pointed at the screen. Pantelis moved past her and attempted to turn off the TV.

'Don't, Pantelis, she was talking to me,' said Gillianne. As she stepped back to let Pantelis pass by, she stumbled and fell onto the sofa.

'Don't watch it!' said Pantelis, 'You crazy?'

Gillianne remained on the couch. She had angered Pantelis but did not understand why. Pantelis felt guilty for shouting at her, but it was out of frustration, of not being able to make sense of what was happening to his wife.

Breakfast was silent. Pantelis drank some tea, prepared his lunch—a lump of bread, some salt and onion—and went to work, his thoughts consumed with Gillianne. At lunchtime, he mounted his bike and cycled home to see what she was doing. Gillianne was not at home.

'*Perhaps she has gone to the shops,*' he thought, not quite believing it. He grabbed a cup of tea, gulped it down and went out again. On his way back to work, his eyes combed the pavement on each side of the road—no sight of Gillianne.

At four o'clock, he pulled off his overalls, hopped on his bike and raced back home. Gillianne was still out. Pantelis was worried now. He paced up and down the living room, frequently stopping at the bay window in their front room, looking through the lace curtains which Gillianne kept spotlessly clean. By five o'clock, he was concerned. He wondered if perhaps she was sitting in the park outside Tottenham Town Hall. She did not shop very often as Pantelis took care of that on Friday evenings. But on occasions when she went running errands on the high street, she liked to stop there a while. Mounting his bike again, he raced to The Green by the Town Hall. No Gillianne!

At home within twenty minutes, he stayed up all night waiting for her to return. He phoned the police who said there were no 'accident reports involving a woman of that description.' The admissions list at the local hospital had no record of anyone by the name of Gillianne Kashodis. He waited.

Gillianne had wandered off soon after Pantelis had left for work. She had made her way to Tottenham Green, taken a left turn at the lights after Bruce Grove station and walked through the grounds of Bruce Grove Castle for a while. Eventually, she ended up at Whitehart Lane. Turning left, she reached the Civic Centre on Green Lanes and sat opposite it, on a bench, confused. She sat there all day and then all night, weary of drunk men passing by, her mind ablaze with bad thoughts. Mini-skirted teenagers laughed at her as they passed by, repeatedly turning and looking at her, or so she thought. Two "vagrants," a man and a woman, tried to pull her coat off. She screamed. A young man passing by shouted at the vagrants to leave her alone. They ran off, but Gillian was terrified and began to whimper. A passer-by stopped to help.

'Please call Pantelis. Tell him I need him. Please! Please! Please!' Gillianne was shaking uncontrolled as she repeated these words. Realising Gillianne was confused and afraid; the woman went to the corner phone box and dialled emergency. Before long, two police officers arrived, a policewoman approached her tentatively, careful not to alarm her.

'What's your name, love?'

Gillianne hesitated and then blurted out her name, still sobbing.

'And what's your surname, love?'

'I don't know. Please call Pantelis. Tell him I need him, tell him to come now, please, please, tell him to be quick.'

She could not remember her home number. She searched for it in her confused mind and finally remembered Pantelis' surname. 'Kashodis,' she said, sobbing.

'Can you spell that?'

As always, the question irritated Gillianne, who spelt it rapidly, furiously.

'Don't worry, we will find him,' said the policewoman who took the name down just as quickly.

At ten past four, Pantelis picked up the phone, 'Yes, I am Mr Kashodis… Yes, she is my wife; I couldn't sleep all night. I was waiting for news from the police…Yes, thank you very much. I am waiting for you…143, Stamford Hill Road, Stamford Hill, yes, yes, not far from the supermarket.'

At last, Gillianne was at home. She went to bed and covered her face, trying to shut out the voices telling her "nasty things." When narrating her illness, she often recalled these whispers in her ears and always referred to them as "nasty things." She was cold and frightened. Tucked comfortably In bed, she began to smile; she looked as if she was listening to someone.

She panicked when the voices urged her to run out of the house, to run away and never come back. When she was ill, Pantelis was enemy number one. In a sense, he was, as he had to keep her locked up in the house in case she ran away and was exposed to danger.

'*Locked up in the house, at least she is safe*,' thought Pantelis. The garden was enclosed with high walls and hedges. Pantelis always left the kitchen door unlocked in case of fire but locked the front door and took the keys with him. He knew that she could not climb the high wall.

The illness had changed Gillianne beyond recognition. She put on weight because of the medication she was prescribed to control her moods. When she was on a "high," caring for her and protecting her from danger was a challenge. These episodes of instability became more and more frequent. Pantelis was overwhelmed by her furious energy, which was invariably followed by clinical depression.

'Sometimes, my head spins round and round. She is all around the house, cleaning and cleaning and cleaning,' he would say when he attempted to describe the force of Gillianne's obsessive activities.

At moments like this, when he spoke honestly about his feelings, he sounded as if he was complaining, albeit mildly, about his life with Gillianne. Encouraged by these confessions, his brother's wife Helena would start, 'Why don't you leave her, Pantelis? You haven't been happy since you met her.'

This was an exaggeration. Pantelis had been happy. Gillianne was kind and generous, and when she was well, they had lots of fun and laughter together. He loved her, and she adored him.

In contrast to Gillianne who shook her head from side to side when disagreeing, Pantelis cocked his head back slightly to signal his disagreement. He then made a disapproving sound between his teeth, as Cypriots do, to reinforce his position and establish what he felt were his true feelings. 'Leaving Gillianne is unthinkable.' His face was drawn and determined; his eyes were dilated, sad. 'No, that would not be right,' he said.

'Why not Pantelis? Why do you have to spend your life chasing after a mad *Englesa*? (the mad Englishwoman) She will get worse, you know.'

'Only God knows what the future holds. Anyway, I cannot leave her now. I think it was God's will that we met and married. This is her fate, and it is mine too.' To his Turkish Cypriot friends, he used the word kismet in place of fate. He liked using Turkish synonyms. It made him feel knowledgeable and free from prejudice towards his Turkish Cypriot compatriots.

With these words, his thin lips tightened, his small brown eyes glazed over as he tried to convince others and, even if he was not aware of it, himself too, of the need to stay with Gillianne.

In truth, there were times when Pantelis wondered whether he could go on taking care of her. He would try to stop thinking that he could not, reminding himself of his pledge. Had he not promised to be with her 'in sickness and in health?' That was the promise he had made before God, in that North London Orthodox Church, off Green Lanes. How could he go back on his word? It seemed unthinkable.

Remembering his vows gave him the will to soldier on. In time he grew to accept his fate and to enjoy life when he could. 'I live for the moment,' he would say, smiling with a saint-like serenity. He was philosophical, totally accepting of his fate to stay with Gillianne, dutifully, childless and at least outwardly, without resentment.

***

The couple's childlessness was a sore point and a source of great sadness for Pantelis. Surprisingly, this problem was solved by Gillianne, who one day suggested adoption. At first, she brought the subject up as a way of *"testing the waters,"* as she said to herself—to find out how Pantelis felt about her carrying a baby.

'Pantelis, I don't think we can have a child in my condition. I am taking too many pills. Anyway, this illness is a curse on my family. Look at us; I am ill, my mother was ill. My brother is beyond help.'

Gillianne was in full flow, giving a list of reasons why they should not have a child. The image of her brother, drenched in his urine, sitting in the grimy scullery of a canal boat, drinking, shouting abuse and being generally unwelcoming made her stall. For a second, she reflected on the possibility that her unborn baby might become like her brother, whom she could hardly recognise when they last visited him.

'You saw the way he was, last time we saw him,' she continued, 'a sorry sight, alcoholic, lonely and mad.' She paused before going on, 'His living space is a mess; like a pig-sty. We can't bring a child into this world knowing that he may turn out to be like me—or worse, like him!'

Pantelis remained silent for a minute, although this seemed much longer to Gillianne who, despite what she said, hoped that Pantelis would say they could take a chance. Pantelis spoke thoughtfully, unaware of Gillianne's feelings.

'If we didn't know, *agapi mou,*' he said, his eyes fixed on the floor, 'and the child was born and had this condition, then it would be fate. But we do know, and there's a fifty-fifty chance he or she will be born with this condition.' He said the word she as an after-thought, a remote possibility that if they had a child, it could be a girl. 'It would be wrong to bring a baby into this world to suffer what you and some members of your family are having to endure.' He paused to see Gillian's reaction to his reasoning.

Gillianne was uncharacteristically silent. She had hoped that Pantelis would dismiss her comments and perhaps say, 'If it is God's will, we can find the strength to bear it.' But as much as she wanted to carry a child and be a mother, she also wanted to have a healthy child. Pantelis' comments sounded final, though, and put an end to her hopes. That night she wept quietly and for a long time. Tears ran down her ruddy, plump cheeks, wetting the pillow. Every time she changed the bed linens, she remembered the pronouncement that she would be barren all her life.

'*Like a heifer,*' she thought, '*I will remain barren, and only good for the chopper.*'

She had grown up in the countryside on a farm and knew about animals. The image of a sad-eyed heifer awaiting the slaughterhouse reflected her low self-esteem—sometimes to the point where she wanted to slit her wrists and bleed to death. '*Death would be a relief,*' she thought, misquoting Shakespeare as she shook with tears, bemoaning her desolation, her loneliness.

Not long afterwards, on a Sunday morning when she was feeling quite well and had a more positive outlook on her life with Pantelis, she spoke again about children.

'I think you are right, Pantelis. We don't need to remain childless.'

She said this as she sat down to have breakfast with him. Tomatoes, cucumber, olives, hellim cheese, toast, and eggs were all laid out on the table with some butter and bergamot jam. The tea was warm and welcoming. Pantelis filled his cup and added three teaspoons of sugar. He loved this jam that his mother had made from their bergamot oranges. Its pleasant jasmine-like aroma filled the room.

***

The night before bringing up the topic of children, Gillianne had been talking to herself. In fact, "reasoning" with herself would better describe it, as she quite regularly spoke to herself. Often, and self-deprecatingly, she joked about talking to people inside the television and conversing with persons no one else could see. But that night she reasoned with herself as if she were two people. Her critical self was brutal and uncompromising. The little girl in her answered meekly and tried to justify her actions. The powerful self was sometimes her grandmother or her mother. At other times, it was God. Gillianne, too, was religious. She had converted to the Orthodox denomination when she married Pantelis. Every Sunday, they prayed together for Gillianne to get better and thanked the Lord for the food and comfort they were provided.

'I have been thinking,' she continued. 'If I can bring myself to hold another woman's child and call him mine, then we can share the joy of bringing up a boy. Surely I can do that!' As she spoke, there were tears in her eyes and a pain in her heart.

She knew they could not adopt in the UK because of her health. The state, rightly, tried to ensure that people who adopted were in good health and financially stable. Gillianne agreed that children had to be protected and was in fact, unsure whether she could safely raise a child. But she knew that Pantelis could and would take care of the child and keep him safe when she became ill.

In the past, she was unable to accept Pantelis' proposal to adopt a baby boy. This morning she felt differently.

'Pantelis, I have thought long and hard about this. I think it would be nice to adopt a boy and to care for him.'

Pantelis glanced at her with that searching look that Gillianne knew so well. She knew he was wondering whether she was on a high again.

'*She can't be! She has just recovered from an attack*,' he thought, as he sat back and observed her, his eyes half-closed, quizzical.

After some minutes, he spoke, 'Are you serious? Gillianne, what made you change your mind?'

'Pantelis, my love, I wasn't totally against adopting. It is just that I know the authorities are strict about adoption, and it would have been disappointing to apply and be turned down. Especially for you, as I know you would like to adopt a baby.' She paused for a few seconds and then continued, 'But last year, when we visited the orphanage in Limassol to see your cousin's boy, you know, Dimitris, I began to warm to the idea. He needs a family. I have thought that I would like to be his mother if they would let us adopt him. Of course, I am not sure whether the authorities here would allow it, but I suppose we can find out.'

Gillianne did not say that she had observed Pantelis' longing to parent that child when they visited the orphanage. His face had glowed with excitement and expectation. She knew he wanted her to say she would like the boy to be their child too. But deep down, something, she did not know what, had stopped her.

Pantelis' eyes were alight. He looked upwards where he had always imagined God resided and whispered an inaudible, "Thank you." He stood up and walked towards Gillianne.

'My love, I am sure they will consider it! After all, the boy is a relative.' He kissed her on her forehead.

Gillianne was moved. 'I am more worried about the authorities here, to be honest. But if we are lucky and they allow it, I will do my best to be a good mother to him.'

Her eyes glistened with tears. Neither she nor Pantelis was convinced she would be a good mother all the time, but they were sure she would be a loving mother and would be able to demonstrate her love when she was well.

Pantelis told her these thoughts, and as he did, he felt closer to her. Her willingness to adopt despite the difficulties made him love her even more. His conviction that Gillianne was an excellent person reaffirmed itself, and he reached out to her and embraced her. Tears welled up in his eyes too, and to hide his emotion from Gillianne; he held her head against his shoulder. They held onto each other while Pantelis softly stroked her hair.

Before she could change her mind, Pantelis set about writing a letter to the orphanage in Limassol proposing the adoption. Writing an official letter was not easy for him; he struggled with it, and the waste-paper basket was filled with his many unsatisfactory attempts. Unsure of the correct format for formal letters in Greek, he decided that the English format would suffice. He made sure that the addressee's details were written in the top left-hand corner of the letter, his own on the right, neatly indented as was the fashion in letter-writing then.

After introducing himself, he declared that as Dimitris was his relative, he would like to adopt him.

'I am sure that his parents would be pleased if there was any way for them to know that their distant cousin is offering their child a loving home. My wife and I have been unable to have children of our own, and when we visited Dimitris last year, we both felt drawn to him. We feel that his presence in our home will brighten our lives, and it will be a joy to look after him, protect and nurture him into adulthood and support him through his education and training until he can fend for himself.'

He begged them to consider his application urgently and hoped that their decision would be in the affirmative. He signed the letter, held it up to the light to reread it. He then said a prayer. After sealing the envelope, he realised that in his rush to write the letter, he had forgotten about his breakfast and more importantly, awaiting client. He decided to ignore hunger. A storm was forecast for the next day, with gales at 80 miles an hour and torrential rain, a rare event in southern England. He had promised to fix his client's leaking roof before then. He picked up the letter, grabbed a piece of toast, spread some jam on it, said goodbye to Gillianne, hopped on his bicycle and was gone.

It was not long before Dimitris arrived in England. With the child in their home, there was suddenly much joy and happiness. Even Gillianne's health was stable for a while, and Pantelis was elated. He was proud of little Dimitris and always referred to him as a "good boy" even when Dimitri was a grown-up man with children of his own.

***

Gillianne continued her monologue, her voice metallic. 'When I was on a high, I always refused any medication given to me. I was sure I was perfectly ok. It was everybody else that was out of step, not me. I felt enclosed in the house and wanted to get out. Pantelis hated having to lock me in, didn't you Pantelis? But he had to, I suppose; he had to go to work. Locking me in was dangerous; he knew this. But he had no choice. It was either that or I would run out of the house and roam the streets. Sometimes, when I managed to run away, I sat on a bench in some park for hours on end and occasionally, when he could not find me, I slept there.'

This was painful for Sonay to hear, but she was also intrigued. Her mother and patients at the hospital where she worked never discussed how they felt and often refused to take their medicines. Here was a woman who was not only talking about her ill health but reflecting on her behaviour and feelings.

"I have had a lot of help, of course, not like in Cyprus. You know, Pantelis took me to Cyprus once when Dimitris was young. He thought a smaller community would be more caring and accepting, and I would have an easier time of things and be safer during relapses. He was so wrong! They did whatever it took to aggravate me when I was ill. They used to call me *Englesa*.' She paused for breath and then continued, her eyes fixed on the wooden floor.

'There was an old donkey in the field behind the house. Pantelis had rented this house thinking I was more likely to be left alone there. The poor donkey was free to roam the dry fields, but it was constantly abused by the children who played near to our rented house. They beat her with sticks, kicked her, chased her around the field till she was exhausted. The kicking and beating went on and on, and I could not stand watching such cruelty; I went outdoors and chased the children away. Then I brought the poor donkey into our walled garden where she would be safer.'

Remembering this episode in her life, Gillianne became sad. Her speech was punctuated with nervous, hysterical laughter that turned to tears.

'The women in the neighbourhood thought I was crazy to be running after an old donkey, all day long. If I took the donkey to another spot in the open fields so she could feed herself better, their children followed, taunting me. There wasn't the slightest attempt by parents to stop their wrong-doings. They joined in.'

'Where are you taking her Gillianne? You have nothing else to do but tend to a diseased donkey?'

The children followed me about and chanted, 'Gillianne, Gillianne, the mad *Englesa* with her smelly donkey and her smelly knickers! Where are you taking her?'

'But I carried on anyway. They were not friends, you see. The donkey was an excuse for them to get at me.' Gillianne's eyes began to tear as she remembered her loneliness. She felt she had been lonely all her life, shunned by everyone except Pantelis, and a few of his friends.

Sonay remembered that her mum had many friends. She was loyal to all as they were to her. This contrast, she felt must have been due to the tendency of people to want to exclude those around them who are different, and Gillianne looked different in that neighbourhood. In London, her isolation may have been caused by the nature of life in the metropolis.

'They don't have the same attitude towards animals as we do over here, do they, Panteleimon?' she said trying to distance herself from, forget about, the year she spent in Cyprus.

Pantelis nodded in agreement, and Gillianne continued, 'And they were cruel to humans too. They were cruel to me. I was always the outsider, the odd one out, wasn't I, Pantelis?' Pantelis agreed, but privately he thought it a bad idea for Gillianne to remember, and dwell on, the past. She was already in a state. There was no need to indulge in remembering things that would upset her even more. Predictably, she started to cry again.

'Why are you crying now? It is all in the past. Long forgotten,' said Pantelis, trying to console her.

'It didn't work out for me,' sobbed Gillianne. 'I felt they were all against me, and I hated living there.'

Pantelis was embarrassed and gazed down at his polished brown shoes. He stood up and straightened his trousers, the fawn-coloured pair he always wore when he went out.

Sonay looked at Gillianne, and she thought about her dear mother, who also often walked out of the house with no word to anyone, returning some hours later. Even when she was well, she often said she felt like running away, 'falling into a road and then just going on and on.' These words frightened Sonay when she was a child; they made her feel unloved. And she even blamed herself whenever her mum took off, left the house, left the family to stay with relatives for a few days. When she was older, she joined in the search for her missing mum, who, unlike Gillianne, was with a relative or close friend. On the way to and from these visits, she never provoked verbal abuse. Listening Gillianne's ordeal in Cyprus saddened her.

Recalling her time in Limassol reminded Gillianne of her daughter-in-law. This was why she had become more upset, as she was not pleased with the girl who had disrupted their happy family. Dimitris' marriage to Stella had been arranged, and so Stella left Cyprus and her family to live with him in London. Stella had an uncompromising personality. She expected to have fun, go out and enjoy herself. This was London and living in London was one reason that she had agreed to marry Dimitris; she imagined a glittering life of luxury. But Dimitris was a quiet, even-tempered young man who was content with life and with his parents. He found Stella's tumultuous personality frightening, and she found him to be dull.

'You are only young once. You can't sit at home all day listening to your mum saying the same things. It is boring! I am bored. Can't you see I am bored?' Stella's eyes widened with anger as she said this to a cowering Dimitris, who had soon realised this violent streak in Stella and was wary of her. Curiously, he liked her bossy, definitive attitude. She excited him, in a way he could not understand.

'I work all day! I am tired, I need to rest,' he countered meekly. This was enough to send Stella into a rage. She had a mop of black curly hair, which she tossed violently when she got angry. Her large almond-shaped eyes, the only attractive part of her round, fleshy face, grew wide as she threatened violence. She was short with a square body and stumpy, muscled legs. Her calves resembled those of a weight-lifter in training. She spoke loudly and confidently and had an opinion on everything and would defend it to death. In this, she was like killer birds, determined to win or die but never to give in. She considered giving in to be a sign of weakness, and Dimitris, in so far as she could tell, was a wimp. Unlike her, he put everyone else before himself. He lived with his elderly parents in harmony, always going along with whatever they wanted to do, never contradicting them. She was maddened to see him bow to every suggestion or command that came from Gillianne, not realising that this was the only way Dimitris could manage her changing moods. For Stella, there was one way to deal with Gillianne, and that was to 'stand up to her.'

'I can't live here,' she said. 'Don't expect me to live with your parents all my life. Are you not a man? Do you not have the guts to stand up to them, set up your own house and live apart from them? I married you, not your parents, and I may well regret having done so. I am not spending my life living with them.'

With this, she stomped around the room and then stood by the window, looking out but not seeing. Suddenly, she noticed the rain outside, a drizzle that went on incessantly.

'It's always raining in this bloody country,' she said, feeling caged.

Dimitris went over to her, tentatively reaching out to touch her shoulder, calm her down so that they could talk reasonably. Stella rebuffed him.

'Oh, leave me alone. I am not interested. You know what? I think you are boring. I am not going to stay here and live the life of a slave. I am used to much better things than this. Go to hell!'

Dimitris had grown fond of Stella by now. He was twenty-one years old, and this was his first close contact, relationship with a woman other than his mother. He liked her smell. At night when they made love, he felt all the tension in his body released. He was happy to be with her. He loved her; he even loved her temper and, interestingly, rather enjoyed being bossed about by her. But setting up their own home would be expensive. On his present wages, he could not afford to do this.

Stella's English was not good, but she was ambitious. She had trained as a pediatric nurse and wanted to work in her field. She was not prepared to take on menial work to supplement Dimitris' income so that they could save up to buy or even rent a flat. Besides, she knew that Pantelis had a lot of money. At least, that's what she thought on the day of the proxenia, when Pantelis proposed to her parents that Stella and Dimitris be married. Stella remembered the little man sitting on the edge of their 'luxurious' (as she called it) chair in their living room. Her father had started a business which was doing well, and the lavishly furnished room was a reflection of their new wealth. Pantelis blinked at the sight of the ornate, gilded Italian furniture. He sat on the edge of the large chair lest he disappeared into its depths and smiled at his host, accepting their hospitality before embarking on the business of arranging a marriage for his son.

'He is a good boy, my Dimitris, hard-working and modest. He is a good bricklayer and gets on famously with everyone.' He omitted the fact that Dimitris had no friends and continued to praise him.

Dimitris was indeed a "boy." Even when he spoke, he sounded like a child. An observant eye would have easily spotted his naivety, especially at this moment when the situation warranted a man. He sat close to his father; he was feeling sticky and uncomfortable in his new suit on this hot and humid evening. All-day long, he had roasted in the sun as they wandered throughout the bazaar. His father insisted that he wore a suit, so they bought this one from a shop close to the *pantopoulio*. Because it was new, it did not feel comfortable, and he was not used to wearing suits anyway. Here he was, feeling flushed, blushing at his father's compliments. He was always embarrassed by his father's exaggerated praise. Whenever they were visiting relatives or friends, Pantelis always ended with the phrase typical of a doting father, 'He is a good boy, my Dimitris.'

Stella had a sharp eye, and she could sense Dimitris' malleable nature under the shiny ill-fitting suit. She thought if the marriage went ahead, it would not be too difficult to manage this rather handsome but childlike man. She became excited as she imagined herself in his arms, walking down the promenade in Paphos or wandering around shops in London while he patiently waited on her. Yes, if the father had money, she could get along with Dimitris just fine. She knew the father had a lot of money. Her father had told her so.

But Dimitris felt obliged to stay near his family and help his father, especially giving him moral support when Gillianne was ill.

'What's wrong with living here? The house is comfortable, and we have a room of our own. I love you. We can live here happily.'

Then as an afterthought, he said, 'Don't worry about Mum. Dad and I will handle her.' This enraged Stella even more, and she stomped out of the room deliberately slamming the door, knowing that this would annoy Gillianne who straight away was at the door, glaring at Stella. Confrontations like this had become regular events in the household.

'Go ahead, carry on like this, my girl, carry on! Never mind the doors. Just break them. I hope you brought enough money from your dad to repair the damage you cause in this house.'

'Oh, shut up, you old bat.'

'I may be old and mad, but at least I respect my husband—which is more than I can say for you.'

'Oh, shut up!' said Stella angrily. She hated Gillianne, and this was clearly written on her contorted face. 'I am not a prisoner here. I have come to be with my husband who is still in your clutches, you witch!'

'We have given you plenty, more than you deserve! Dimitris is too nice to stand up to you, and you take advantage of him.'

'What's plenty? Something to eat? Water from the tap? I am used to more than that. Don't worry; I will leave soon. You can have your beloved son back!'

At this point, Gillian decided to change tact, play things down. She did not want to be responsible for their separation.

'Anyway, stop slamming the doors. We paid good money for them.' Gillianne was now using her 'posh English.' She often used her 'posh accent' to establish her superiority. Stella was communicative in English but spoke it with a strong, throaty accent typical of Greeks.

***

Gillianne came from a cultured family. Her father had some land in Hampshire and was said to be descendent of an earl, though he did not inherit his land from his father. It was left to him by his great aunt; or rather, she had left him some money that he invested in a small "farm." While the farm could not provide for the family, he loved the countryside and thought the land gave him some status in their small village. But he neglected the land, and in the end, it was used to graze a variety of animals and became more like zoo than a farm. Some Scottish cows, an unbroken white horse, twenty or so Angora goats and about fifteen sheep who multiplied in the winter months, a donkey rescued from Brighton beach, a few hens, some rabbits, and a lama that a visiting circus left him. Its leg was injured and much to the delight of Gillianne, her father, offered it home until the circus returned the following year. In the end, the llama was never claimed and remained as the mascot of the smallholding.

Had he been at all enterprising, he might have opened the farm to the public; perhaps to schools, for educational visits. But he was not, and the farm continued to run at a loss. Eventually, property developers bought the land very cheaply at auction. Gillianne was naturally less than pleased with this outcome, and she rarely visited her parents, who were given a small house on the property by the developers.

Stella was insisting that the marriage was not working out.

'I am going to leave you, Dimitris. I can't take your mum anymore,' she said one evening when Dimitris returned home tired from work.

'Why, what happened today then? Weary, but by now used to her daily list of complaints, he sat on the edge of the chair, careful not to soil it with his dirty work clothes. This reaction was enough to send Stella into another rage— an event familiar to the whole household. She stormed out of the bedroom, but, this time, she did not slam the door. Dimitris followed her into the kitchen and held her from behind, tried to console her as she began to sob. The stern expression she usually wore on her face had changed into a sad, pitiful look, her eyes filled with tears and her mouth contorted as she tried to control her crying.

'I am tired of all the arguments in this house,' she said sobbing.

The truth was that she missed her own family, which she realised as soon as she heard her mother's voice earlier that day. She had decided to call her mother to tell her that she wanted to leave Dimitris. She knew that she wanted to be with her own family and craved the freedom she was used to in Limassol.

Having little money, she raided the change box in the kitchen, took all the 10p coins and walked quickly to the closest phone booth.

Her mum answered the phone, pleased to hear her daughter's voice.

'We are fine, Stella mou,' said Eleni in response to Stella's query.

'I want to come home, Mum. This thing isn't working.'

'What thing? What isn't working, Stella mou?' Eleni was peeling a head of kolokassi, a potato-like root vegetable, and the shock made her drop the knife, which cut into her toe rather deeply. Eleni listened to Stella, not letting on that she had just had an accident. She wanted to stay calm and advise her daughter that things would settle in time. But Stella's trembling voice and unhappy state made her change her mind.

'If you are that unhappy, Stella mou, just pack your bags and come home. I'll tell your daddy to send you your ticket and some money to travel back.'

Before she could say any more, the line was cut off. As she began to clean the wound, she went over and over in her mind, the circumstances leading to the marriage. They had sent their daughter to a household about which they knew nothing and expected her to get on with it. She had thought it was unwise then and had argued with her husband. But Stella's father put his foot down, stating that he 'trusted Pantelis one hundred per cent.' Indeed, he was right to do so, but this wasn't about Pantelis. It was about personal relationships and Stella's ability to manage them. Eleni knew her daughter well, and her mother's intuition told her that Stella wasn't mature enough for marriage. She tried in vain to convince her husband to change his mind. Quite naturally, Stella was excited about living in London. She thought Dimitris was handsome and he seemed easy to get along with. Besides, she had always dreamt of a life of luxury. Such life in London was a bonus. The decision was sealed.

Stella arrived back at the house, and locked herself in the heaven of her bedroom and began to pack. When she finished, she carefully placed the case under the antique iron bed that she hated and picked up a book to read while she waited for Dimitris. She did not go down into the kitchen for lunch, and by four-thirty when Dimitris came home, she was starving.

'What is it, my love? Have you not eaten at all today?'

'I want to go back home, Dimitris. I have had enough. I miss my family. I am going to go back to them. If you want to live with me, then you will have to come to Limassol. You have a good trade. I am sure you will be able to get a job there.'

'Ok, ok, don't cry now.' He drew her close to him and

kissed her eyes. He was falling in love with her, and she knew it. That evening, they ate their dinner alone. Gillianne had gone out, and Pantelis had gone to look for her. They sat together in the kitchen and mapped out a plan. Stella would return to Cyprus, and Dimitris would follow her within a month. Although he had a steady job with the Council with good prospects, he would give it up to follow Stella. He was sure he would not be dissuaded from this, their first joint decision because he knew with absolute certainty that he loved Stella.

Gillianne was enraged. 'Dimitris, just let her go. She is not worth it. Can't you see that?' Who was this woman, who had come out of nowhere and within weeks was planning to take her beloved Dimitris away? And her son! He seemed all set to leave London, his job, his parents and all he knew to follow her to Cyprus, to live in a country he barely understood.

Pantelis watched Dimitris for a long time and said little. Occasionally he would remark that it was, in fact, their lives and they had a right to live it the way they wanted to. But he was concerned about Dimitris. *He is a nice boy but rather inexperienced. How would he manage to live with his in-laws and still maintain his dignity?* This question repeated itself over and over in his mind, and then finally, he spoke about his concerns with Dimitris.

'Dimitri *mou*, living with in-laws is not the same as living with your parents. You will be without a job, maybe for a long time. Limassol is not the same as in London.'

'Oh dad, do you think I haven't thought of that? It is on my mind all the time. But I have fallen in love with Stella. She is the first woman I have been with. I want to stay with her.'

Pantelis remembered his love for Gillianne. He felt he understood the force behind Dimitri's words.

'I understand, my son,' he said and left him sitting in the kitchen. In his bedroom, he took out some paper and a pen and began to write.

Dear Kyriakos,

I have not written to you for a long time but believe me; you are always on my mind. Coming to Cyprus is a joy when I have the good fortune to meet up with you and your family for meals and talks. It reminds me of the old days when we were always together.

Kyriakos, I know that you are busy at your shop. You were telling me this. I thought that you might need a helping hand. My Dimitris is now married, you know. His wife, Stella, came to London but could not get on with things. It is difficult for her—a strange country, learning another language, no relatives around, and of course, I do not have to hide it from you, some difficulties at home. Anyway, they have decided to live in Cyprus and Dimitris will be leaving London within a month. Stella will return, and Dimitris will follow her after he has worked out his resignation with the Council. He has a good job there with good prospects, but he will have to hand in his resignation. Naturally, I am concerned that he will come to Limassol and have to live with his in-laws. He will need a job to help him to maintain his dignity, and I do not think he will be able to get a job straight away. It may take him months. I am wondering if you would be willing to let him come and work with you.

Please do not misunderstand. I do not want you to pay

him a wage. I will pay his wages every month to you, and you can pay him with that money. One thing I will ask from you: Please let this be a secret between us. Dimitris is a proud boy. He will be hurt if he knows I have made a deal with you.

My boy is a good man. You will like him. If you do, maybe we can expand your business and make him a partner. I have money saved to help set him up and what better way to invest it than in the business of my trusted friend who, I know, works hard and is very capable.

Please let me know what you think.

Ps. Sorry, in a rush to sort things out, I have forgotten to ask about Evgenia and the children. I hope they are all well. Please give them my love and best wishes.

I look forward to getting your letter soon.

In the meantime, minete me to kalo.

Your friend,
Pantelis

Pantelis got up from his desk and looked out the window. He could see Gillianne in the distance, standing at the traffic lights, likely confused and lost. She appeared to be having an intense conversation with someone, except that she was alone. Pantelis locked the sealed envelope in his desk drawer and ran out, praying that Gillianne would remain where she was. As he approached the intersection, Gillianne was still standing there, arguing with an imaginary opponent. He reached out, gently touching her on the shoulder, and took her hand, tugging at it reassuringly.

'Let's go home, my love.'

Gillianne usually resisted him when she was ill, but now she tagged along without objecting. Together they returned home, where Pantelis helped her to lay down on the bed. He then went to get her pills and some water. Gillianne looked exhausted. Within the hour, she was fast asleep and snoring heavily as she did when she took these pills. For a few minutes, Pantelis watched her sleeping, shaking his head as he repeated, 'Kaimeni mou, kaimeni mou.' He then unlocked the desk drawer, took the letter out, put a stamp on it, looked up and said a prayer and went out to post it.

***

Dimitris' departure for Limassol left a big gap in his parents' lives. Gillianne and Pantelis made several trips to Cyprus to visit him. They stayed in Pantelis' village, where he busied himself renovating the cottage his mother had bequeathed him in her will, while Gillianne cleaned obsessively. Dimitris occasionally visited when he found time from work and his family commitments-and when Stella agreed. He was now a proud father of two lovely girls and a boy. '*Thio kores ge'nan bethin*,'[4] he would say, as most Greek Cypriots do, unaware of the discriminating tone in this expression. He was also a significant partner in a construction company. The business was expanding fast in southern Cyprus. New hotels were being built to meet the ever-increasing tourist demand.

'He is ok, our Dimitri. He has settled well in Limassol and is a good family man now,' said Pantelis, on one of their visits to Sonay's family. Gillianne had not been well since

---

4 Two daughters and a child – it is assumed that child is a boy.

Dimitris left. She was less talkative now and was continually massaging the area just above her left breast, complaining of chest pains.

'I lost count of the number of pills I was taking, so now I take my medication monthly through an injection. It is better this way. I don't forget it and remain well for most of the time.' This was how she had described her health on her last visit. Otherwise, she remained silent.

***

When Sonay and Akay returned home from work, they were both tired and hungry. It was a late autumn evening when the days were shortest. The long drive home was exhausting, as it had rained all day and the light reflecting on the puddles in the road made driving hazardous. Their home, like that of Pantelis, was empty now. Their girls were at university, and the piano had been silent throughout autumn. The large house echoed nothing more than short business-like conversations between the two people who said little, each afraid to upset the other.

Akay began to prepare the supper while Sonay went to check for telephone messages. Of the two recorded messages, the first was indecipherable. The second was the familiar voice of Pantelis.

'Gillianne has died, she is dead,' he said.

The voice caught on the telephone, suggested an emotion Pantelis wanted to keep private. Then he hung up.

Outside, the rain intensified. November, 'The month of the drowned dog'[5] raged with fury. Sonay thought of the many homeless and poor out in the rain. The tramp hud-

5 Ted Hughes – November - Lupercal (1960)

dling beneath his coat in Ted Hughes' poem symbolised for her the many who, unable to live as others, fell out and fell off. Maybe Gillianne was lucky. She was certainly luckier than most. Pantelis had never abandoned her, and she had never fallen off.

Sonay tried to visualise Gillianne's last moments. She wondered if she had thanked Pantelis for taking care of her and for enduring all the hardships she had brought to their marriage. Had she remembered to tell him, as she often did, that she was sure he would go to heaven? Did she laugh in that familiar shrill voice that would have made Pantelis think—at least momentarily-that she had returned to a "normal" state of mind?

Had she closed her eyes and gone to sleep, never to wake up again? Or was it more violent than that, struggling before giving up, giving in?

The rain had become a storm. Lightning was followed by thunder, lighting up the kitchen and the room where Sonay sat quietly, remembering the night her mother had died. She got up from the sofa, closed the curtains and wished for her children to be with her, next to her. Seated by the fire, the warmth made her feel drowsy, and soon she was asleep, dreaming of her mother, feeling guilty still for not having taken her to a doctor on that day when her mother held her breast and said it felt hard.

It was no consolation to learn that her mother's illness was already too far advanced, nor to know that she had other relatives living with her who might have noticed sooner. As a daughter, she had always felt it her duty alone to take care of her gentle, sensitive, loving mother; she missed so much. Her mother became Gillianne and Gillianne her mother as she dreamt on, crying real tears. She slept deeply, unaware that Akay had come into the room, covered her with a blanket, and gone to bed.

The storm raged throughout the night.

In the morning, the skies were clear and bright, and the ancient oak at the base of the garden lay on the ground, uprooted.

***

Patryk

'Are you missing Stanley, Patryk?' Akay asked this as a way of including him into their conversation. He knew that if he didn't try, John would take the stage. For John, conversations were monologues, the topic nearly always politics, analogy through tabloid press regurgitation. His arguments were rarely coherent, and he seemed not to be concerned with the discomforts of dissonance. And yet, he was a good man and was quick to cleverly assess situations and guard against potential danger. This mismatch of capability and his inability to apply it to his political analogy had always been an irritation to Akay.

Patryk was Stanley's housemate. John knew him through Stanley with whom he had once worked on a film set. They had both held principal roles which were cut out at the editing stage so that in the end, each was seen in just one sweeping shot. In retirement, Patryk and Stanley along with John and some other senior citizens, had formed a group and went for walks in Epping Forest. That they were living in the same area in east London was a coincidence.

John shifted uncomfortably in his seat, not because he felt this would cut him out of the 'conversation' he was trying to instigate but because he was concerned about Patryk's well-being. It had been two years since Patryk had suffered a breakdown. His recovery was prolonged because of a sudden bereavement. John did not want him to engage in reminiscing about the past because he was afraid Patryk may have a relapse.

'Yes, terribly,' said Patryk, mono-syllabically, in a barely audible, weak voice. A bad start thought Akay. He believed that talking about personal issues were a good thing and relieved troubled people from deeply seated sorrow, enabled them to better cope with unresolved issues. However, it occurred to him that it may be dangerous to meddle with Patryk's murky past. After all, he knew so little about the man. John is right he thought. Patryk should not be encouraged to bring up issues he may not be able to manage. Still on Patryk's road, they were silent. At the T junction Akay steered the car to the left.

John was going to be eighty in December. He was in the middle of selling his house and was undecided about where to move. He had lived in London for the most part of his life and had been a close friend to Akay. He became a family friend after Akay's marriage. Akay, had retired a while ago. In fact, three years ago he calculated, feeling surprised at how quickly time passes.

Traffic was at a stand-still. This annoyed him. He suffered from periodic depression ever since his youth and in old age this was threatening his health. In the past, he had managed it by busying himself when he was well and taking it easy, allowing his low mood to take its course when he felt down.

John was irritated by Akay's disposition and often went on about the need for him to 'pull himself together.'

'You have a loving family, two lovely children who love you dearly and a wife who cares for you. You have no financial concerns. What have you got to be depressed about?' he would say whenever he noticed Akay's change of mood.

What, indeed, were the issues that depressed Akay? There was no denying that John's list rung true and Akay was aware of his good fortune in this respect. But psychological well-being did not feed on affluence and family support alone. '*It's typical of John to assess things purely at this level,*' he thought.

Talking about his feelings, anxieties, and losses and the effects of all these on his melancholy self, was not an easy task for Akay. His face, seemingly calm, reflected a lifetime of sadness inscribed in the lines that had deepened on his forehead. At such times, he could barely smile. 'How could I begin to respond to a question at this level,' he thought, whenever it was posed and chose to change the subject.

Irritated, John would complain to no avail, 'You never listen to anything I say. I am just trying to help, that's all!'

***

John had been a child star, had a successful career on stage and often topped the bill. He earned a lot during high seasons when his singing was in demand and for the rest of the time, he worked the clubs. These he found 'soul-destroying' and he longed to return to the stage but the seasonal work in winter and summer months was getting harder to find, each year.

He worked with different theatrical companies and directors and as his stagecraft developed his fans grew in numbers. But variety theatre was losing its popularity. Change was inevitable. Pop singers began to dominate the music scene and as he did not try to reinvent himself, or maybe did not know how to do it, he remained dependent on his contracts from Music Halls which became shorter each year.

Women liked John a lot and he enjoyed the attention, but he was more involved with his music. As he travelled up and down the country, doing the clubs and fulfilling seasonal contracts, he had little time to focus on love and marriage until he met Moira in the musical show Brigadoon at the Theatre Royal in Glasgow in which they shared the principal roles. The two matched each other perfectly in singing and soon after in private life. Together, they sung on radio shows and were cast in several pantomimes in Dundee, Ayre and Largs. Love flourished between them but was abruptly extinguished by cancer.

Devastated, John moved to London to improve his job prospects. Alas, his agent was able to find him only occasional work on film sets, some one-night engagements, short television advertisements and such like but nothing more. Scotland continued to offer him parts in ever-decreasing seasonal work in pantomime shows in winter and six-week variety shows in its seaside resorts. Unashamedly, his agent claimed a percentage fee on these too even though they were offered to him through his own contacts. Being John, he was enraged at the unfairness of the system in show business but didn't dare to complain in case he lost all.

In his youth, he was a tall and good looking young man with light blue eyes that were widely set apart mirroring an openness of character. He was jovial most of the time. The long periods of unemployment bored him 'to tears.' In middle age, he maintained his good looks but tended to put on weight and had to go on severe diets to get into shape before major contracts. In his old age, he was still carrying himself majestically.

John often talked of his humble beginnings in Glasgow's infamous 'gorbols.'

'I grew up in a single end,' he would say. 'Do you know what that means? A room and a small opening for a kitchen. A single end for five of us, my mother and father and my two brothers. People were spotlessly clean in these tenements. Not like today with blocks of flats where the lifts and stairs reek of urine. Disgusting! People took turns to clean the stairs and the landings and if anyone missed their turn, they would find their neighbours at their door, wanting to know why the cleaning hadn't been done.'

John had a strong operatic voice, a tenor who sung within his range but equally belt out modern love songs mostly of the fifties and early sixties. As a young man he was offered the chance of training with an opera company in London but he turned it down to stick with his career in music halls and variety shows as well as occasional radio and tv appearances. These brought him fame which he enjoyed. In his later years, he regretted this but did not dwell on it.

In London during a quiet stretch when no work seemed to come his way and winter closed in, to pass the time, he had enrolled on a history course near where he lived. It was a subject he had enjoyed at school, and he was sure it would be a good way to pass the time.

It was on this course that he had met Akay who was elated to have become acquainted with a famous singer. Akay was keen to train as an actor but was too shy to put himself forward. He came to London to study but ended up working in a factory. In the evenings, he attended classes in the hope that he may amass the qualifications needed, to read English and Drama. He was chuffed that he had met someone connected to the theatre and so started their friendship that was to last a lifetime.

Akay smiled at his resolve to prevent John from dominating any discussion that may have started. In the past, he had enjoyed conversing with him. Then, he regarded him as an idol but also a man of the world from whom he felt he learnt a great deal. He had been in London only for a couple of years and knew very little about it. He decided to direct questions at Patryk in the hope that he may inject a new dimension to the imminent conversation in the next hour and a half when the three would be having lunch at a pub along the Forest beyond Chingford.

Akay knew direct questioning was a bad approach in encouraging involvement but felt he had no time to apply other well-tried and tested skills to engage Patryk who was now studying his knees as he sat fingers clasped, in the back seat of his old Ford. 'It sounds like you had a difficult time,' said Akay after a while, not expecting a response from Patryk.

They were climbing Chingford Mount and the old car began to grind halfway up the hill causing Akay to change to a lower gear just when a driver on a side turning, seized the opportunity to join the main road thus causing him to further reduce speed, abruptly. John complained that Akay's driving made him nervous.

'Why are you accelerating when you should be slowing down?' he bellowed showing intense irritation and fear. Akay had indeed accelerated to prevent the engine from stalling. He smiled at his friend's concern for his life at the age of eighty, which he felt far surpassed his own. To take John's mind off the road, he steered his attention to his upcoming relocation.

'What is it that unsettles you?' he asked. 'Is it the move or the money you are laying out on a two-bed retirement flat when a one-bedroom in South Woodford would have sufficed just as well?'

'I don't know, I don't know really,' was John's reply. For a while, he remained subdued.

The car moved on at a leisurely pace through the Ridgeway. On each side of the road, there stood, large, detached houses the regularity of which was broken by blocks of flats, incongruent to the general structure of the buildings in the area. Whenever Akay passed through this road, he was reminded of the British class structure, seemingly as solid as the caste system which the empire had tried to dismantle on the Indian subcontinent. '*Try as it may, socialism would never take root in this country,*' he thought.

Ironically, Marx believed that the UK as the first industrialised country, would lead the way in establishing socialism, and eventually, communism. His theory asserted that this would be an inevitable development caused by the nature of capitalism, characterised by greed. Greed that would impoverish the workers, render them no other choice than to 'overthrow their oppressor' and establish a new egalitarian social order. Impatiently, however, he and his sponsor Engels, anxious to speed the process, decided to campaign outside factory gates and in the end feel disillusioned with the people in whom they had invested their trust to procure the revolution. Now, in the twenty-first century, his tomb in Highgate Cemetery was being spoiled by the fascists. Not that he would care. He was an atheist who regarded religion as the 'opiate of the masses.' Just then, an image of Marx laughing at the wasted efforts of a group people in that amorphous scene, engaged in writing graffiti on his tomb, loomed large in Akay's mind. "Some people just can't see what is! Pathetically, they mirror 'False consciousness.'

Don't you fellows know that there is no life after death?" he imagines him saying and he smiles ever so slightly.

Capital compromised on providing social and health care services, by taking a slice from employee's wages and thus, cushioning the impact of greed so that the argument between the capitalists and the workforce was reduced to wage bargaining. Interestingly, even that was curtailed, ironically by the socialist party briefly in power in the mid-sixties, paving the way for those whose interest it is to preserve the existing social order, to put the dagger in by enacting draconic measures to curtail wage bargaining. The trade unions are now rendered powerless within a procedural entanglement and the conservative party, regrettably supported by a significant proportion of the masses, remains in power for generations as if ordained by God.

They were now at the top of Kings Road and turned right onto Station Road. At the traffic lights, by the historic church, Akay steered the car to the left and drove along by the green in which there stood ancient trees shading the row of houses on a slip road. Next to them stood the Assembly Hall and North Chingford Library, their structure, congruent with the rest of the buildings.

At the start of the High Street, a few shops and a couple of supermarkets flanked each side of the road. Being more expensive than hypermarkets, and perhaps the impact of on-line shopping, few of these managed to survive so that 'To Let' signs appeared periodically on their windows and post-boards.

The rest of the shops on Station Rd. offered goods and services, which were expensive and pretentious. The charity shops remained steadfast, responding to the avarice of consumer culture. Further on were the restaurants which seemed to be doing better. Even those offering ethnic food stood their ground, indicating that the initial apprehension of the natives about foreign food, had subsided.

They descended a slight hill and reached the station. On the left, the expanse stretched out some distance and was bordered by the oak trees of Epping Forest now bare of leaves. The open space was misty so that the edge of the forest was a silhouette. The nearest corner of the expanse was turned into a car park and was used by both dog walkers and people out exercising as well as commuters who could not find parking spaces at the Station's car park. The Station on the right was deserted at this time of the day. No doubt the commuters were hard at work in the city.

The slight decent levelled at a crossroad. Akay stopped the car to give way to drivers who were waiting on the side roads for an opportunity to join the main traffic. John, aware that Akay needn't have given way when driving on the main road bawled, 'It is your right of way, why are you stopping.' Akay drove on, ignoring the comment. He had given way because he felt they themselves were not in a hurry.

'*It would be just like John to interfere with the driver's decision,*' he fumed as he revved the car up hill. The road bent to the left bisecting the forest.

They took a sharp turn to the left and into the car park of the Foresters Pub. On the right of the pub, the infamous lodge of Elizabeth Regina stood majestically on a higher ground. A small building by modern standards, it resembled a tower. Below the high ground, were the hunting fields, an even larger expanse or perhaps the continuation of the one they saw earlier. It too was bordered by the oak forest of Epping and was empty, bar a dog with its owner. The dog roamed unresponsive to the calls of his master who stooped to pick up its excrement with presumably a plastic bag and place it in his pocket. Akay smiled, when he remembered the posters in key places of the expanse and walkways, reminding dog owners to pick up after their dogs and dispose of them in bins provided . His smile froze when he remembered his unruly compatriots, hell-bent on destroying the beaches, the picknick areas, the forests and even the towns and cities in which they lived.

At the turning of the fifteenth century, when the ruling Queen took time off to visit this Lodge, game was rounded up from the forest and driven onto the treeless expanse below the lodge for the 'virgin' queen to aim her arrows at, and kill, in between feasting on good food and love.

Queen Elizabeth 1 was queen of England from November 1558 until her death on the 24th March 1603. The lodge was where she came to take a break from State business. She hunted the deer driven from the forest onto the expanse and within range so she could practice her archery skills. She was known to be a good shot. Her attendants stayed on the first floor of the pub, which was like a hotel. The 'Virgin Queen' lodged and dined at the three-story building the middle part of which had no windows. It was on this floor that she aimed at and killed the panic-stricken deer. The young ones were the first to topple and die in ditches circled by the howling hounds.

Apparently, she dined on the ground floor with her closest companions and made love to Lord Essex until he dared to interfere with the affairs of the state. At that point, the 'Virgin Queen' declared that only she, herself as 'The Queen of this realm' can rule. From then on, she ignored the noble lord's protestations of undying love. Lord Essex was rumoured to have been her first and last lover. She never trusted another man after they broke off and focused on ruling the state with an iron rod. She had built a reputation of being a 'fair and just Queen' through the available publicity means of the time but in reality, had more people killed than her tyrannical father and towards the end of her reign, she became an absolute tyrant. She ignored Parliament's collective advice and ruled with unbridled determination and unprecedented abuse of power. Her advisers thought she was obstinate to the extreme!

Akay was sceptical of this account. At a time when women were regarded as the 'property of men, the 'Virgin Queen' could only survive the intrigues of the palace and the constellation of interests surrounding her, by being the obstinate woman that she was. She held on to the throne she believed was her birth right, by being ruthless. She was but 45 years young when she died! That she killed many an ambitious men to survive as a monarch has to be judged against the social position of women in sixteenth century Britain.

This setting seemed to be unaware of the turmoil in the twenty-first century Great Britain, currently dominated by an economic crisis, created by city barons and bankers' greed. The housing market was on the verge of collapse and needed taxpayer's money to salvage it by propping up banks that recklessly lent mortgages. House prices in Chingford, Woodford Green and Buckhurst Hill had rocketed to half a million mark just before the crisis and amazingly were still holding at those prices. In Walthamstow, accommodation was in demand because of its proximity to the city and good transport links. Prices in that area had increased sharply and were still rising. Young people, unable to buy even the smallest of properties, had to rent from ruthless landlords at exorbitant prices. The local authorities had long stopped building social housing and what they had, was sold to occupants under the directive of the so-called 'Iron Lady' a ruthless mouthpiece of Capital.

'Oh, I know this bit of the forest.' said Patryk feebly, 'We used to come here with Stanley.' Silence ensued and, for a moment, Akay was convinced that his statement had triggered off memories. John shifted uncomfortably, signalling to Akay to stop talking in case Patryk's fragile mental well-being was de-stabilised.

'Yes, it's a nice spot,' said Akay absent-mindedly, looking around for a space to park.

'There is a disabled bay. Park there,' said John breaking the silence in the car. He had sensed his friend's hesitation to take up a scarce space, knowing that there may be others less fortunate who could use the bay. 'You have a badge,' said John. 'Use it.' His definite pronouncement forced a decision.

Akay drove into the bay, feeling uncomfortable and reached out for the brown envelope that contained his disability badges, recently granted to ease the burden of travelling to market or a near-by station, connecting him to occasional work he carried out for an examination board.

Inside the pub, they were feeling warmer. Akay noticed the high noise level, the euphoric atmosphere of the regulars, mostly elderly people, some with families celebrating birthdays. Birth dates of elongated lives were marked each year over a meal, with a drink and well wishes, the eyes of the elderly temporarily animated with the joy of being with their loved ones, the contrast with Patryk's dull, tiny, dark brown eyes, stark.

For a while, they were silent, attending to the menu, making their choice.

'The two-course menu for two people at £9 is a reasonable deal,' said John, insisting that Weatherspoon's in lower Chingford was cheaper. Tongue in cheek, Akay suggested that the venue was better, the historic setting uplifting.

When the waiter came to take the orders, Patryk asked for a beer and cited a gammon steak, a pork meal for his lunch, much to the annoyance of Akay who, though not religious, had an aversion to pork products because of his Muslim upbringing. John ordered fish and chips and Akay who rarely ate red meat decided on a steak and ale pie.

The pub was large and of mock Tudor style. Inside, the sitting areas were separated with dark wooden posts within which nested groups of tables and chairs that gave the impression of privacy. The bar facing the seating area was crowded. Further on, the double doors next to the bar and a separate group of tables and chairs led to the sizable garden below which was the large opening now covered with tall coarse grass. The strong wind could be heard howling against the small windows and the modern double doors.

Akay thought of the deer hit by the queen's arrows. Terrified of the dogs snarling around them, they bled to death paralysed in fear. It was the little ones that went first. With the arrow in their flesh, they staggered on the rough grass before they fell onto their knees and finally gave up living. The dogs guarded the kill till the hunter's aids came to collect their master's or mistress', reward. He lost his appetite.

Large plates of food with the drinks arrived soon after, confirming that they had been microwaved. Suddenly, Akay was aware of the heightened noise level in the pub. He was always surprised at the way the natives displayed enjoyment at family gatherings. Their loud laughter seemed to get louder with alcohol intake and always ended abruptly, suggesting a sense of falseness.

John was still talking. About what, Akay did not know as he had stopped listening. The words seemed to make no impact on his hearing. For a while, he sat in a trance. Patryk who sat still was silent. Every so often he would smile baby like at John animated talk. When his plate of gammon and chips arrived he began to eat hungrily and with obvious pleasure.

Akay's lunch was delayed. He decided that he would have another soft drink and offered the same to the others. John opted for another beer, and Patryk followed suit. He went to the bar and ordered the drinks. Back at their table, for a while they were silent again. Even John was quiet. Sensing that Akay may question Patryk further, he kept on shifting on the wheel-back chair, uncomfortably.

He was right. Akay thought he would try again and started prodding Patryk about his past. This time, his child-like face lit up, smiling innocently, nodding, suggesting that it was traumatic. John's anxiety was at its highest. He poked Akay again, this time by kicking his feet under the table, letting him know that it was not a good idea to search so deeply, silently reminding him of Patryk's fragile state of mind.

Patryk began to reminisce, his smile incongruous with what he was about to reveal.

Before the rebound of his illness, in his early seventies, Patryk used to go swimming regularly. Stanley was well into his nineties and did not go out very often. They had met on a film set. Stanley was an actor with a distinguished voice.

In his later years, he was offered jobs voicing children's animation programmes. He could do this sitting down, so it was just the journey he needed to manage.

Patryk was multilingual. He translated official documents from English to Polish and the reverse. Originally, he was from Poland. In his youth, he became mentally ill but recovered quickly after spending some time in one of the ancient monolithic mental hospitals.

Daniel, his brother, took care of him for a while. He was a successful accountant with business contacts and managed to get Patryk some translation work. Translating was a tedious and lonely job. Afraid that Patryk may get ill again, he encouraged him to register with an agency and get some work as an extra in films. He knew Patryk was interested in acting. Such jobs were occasional and suited him very well. It provided him with an opportunity to go out for a day or two every so often and meet other people-socialise. It was on one of these sets that he met Stanley who decided to take him under his wings.

Patryk was a placid young man. He seemed malleable and undemanding. He retained this stance all through his life except when he was ill.

Stanley lived on his own and felt, though not too large, his house would have room for this young man who was some twenty years younger than himself. His several marriages had ended in divorce, and he determined never to marry again. His work took him away for long periods, and it was hard to sustain marital relations under those circumstances. The 'boy' could keep guard of the house while he was away and would contribute to its upkeep. He was a frugal man. This appealed.

Patryk, his eyes fixed on the edge of the table, was talking. Amazed, Akay and John keyed into his softly spoken words, despite the background noise.

'My parents met in Krakow in Poland, where I was born. My father was a black American showman and came to Krakow with a theatre group, a kind of circus without the animals. It was before the second world war. Then he stayed and married my mother, having fallen in love with her. My mother was called Zofia spelt with a Z, my father was Justin Brown. My name ends with ryk as in Patryk and not Patrick. It means noble I think. Not that I am bequeathed with such an honour...but there you go.'

'The man has a sense of humour,' thought Akay.

Patryk continued, 'My parents divorced when I was very young. It was inevitable really, a black man with a white girl in Krakow, before the second world war!'

He was still smiling.

'During the war, my brother and I were taken to the Kraków-Płaszów concentration camp because we were not Arian. I remember being torn away from my mother, who was calling out in desperation, trying to assure us that she would come for us soon. I was too young to remember any detail. My brother, who was older than me, told me all he knew. We were in the camp for a while. I don't remember much of it... Maybe, only that I was hungry and missed my mother. I don't know. Certainly, I was cold. I remember clinging on to my brother. Sometimes he couldn't take it and pushed me away... These are only vague memories. According to my brother, some days later, we were marched to the entrance of another building. My brother did not know what was behind that door. Then, Apparently, the guard on duty, said our name was not on the list so we were not to enter. By sheer luck or maybe my mother's desperate efforts to rescue us, I don't know which, we were released, and brought to the UK.'

He spoke with a clear diction. His speech was carefully modulated. He was still smiling. Then he stopped again.

***

There was silence for what felt like a long time. Akay began to wonder whether he had done the right thing. He regretted being so insistent. Patryk had recently recovered from a relapse of his long-term mental illness and was feeling frail. Before he became ill, his GP had stopped his medication believing that he had been on them for far too long. General practitioners had apparently been instructed to review the prescriptions of people with a history of mental illness as their medication may no longer be effective if taken for long time. He should have replaced it with a different drug but he hadn't. Perhaps he had been misled by Patryk's calm and tranquil appearance and thought he no longer needed the medication. Who knows!

Stanley had noticed the change in his behaviour and had asked what was going on. Patryk, who was now happy that he did not have to take any medication, had said that all was well. The drugs gave him a dry mouth and made him docile. He was happy to be rid of them.

He was keen on swimming and had been in the swimming pool when he felt confused, staying in the water for hours until the lifeguard decided he ought to have gone long ago and had dived in to check what the problem was. The pool was warm, but he had stayed too long in it and his body lost its self-regulated heat. He was cold, shivering. The guard, aware that something must have been wrong, had asked him to come out of the pool. Patryk resisted.

The pool personnel had had to use force to get him out, but all through the struggle, he insisted that he did not want to go anywhere. When at last, he was pulled out of the pool, he felt disorientated, unable to recall his address. With force used on him, his arms were battered, bruised and aching.

The lifeguard had found the telephone number on his records and rung his house. Stanley's trained actor's voice had answered. He was old and frail but said he would be on his way to collect Patryk, appealing to the life guard not to use force, assuring him that he himself would be able to handle the situation. In a rush to get to the pool at his grand age of ninety-five and with acute angina, a heart attack was inevitable. He collapsed outside their terraced house in Walthamstow and ended up at casualty. He died soon after, his final thoughts with his friend and companion, unaware that they had occupied adjacent cubicles in the casualty department. Patryk, at that very moment, was in the process of being transferred to the mental health unit of the same hospital.

It had taken a long time for Patryk to recover and in all that time, he had not known of Stanley's sad end. When he was told, he would not accept it. He should have noticed that Stanley had not visited him, but just then he was not able to judge the seriousness of it. He was unaware of time and was still agitating with staff, locking himself in the bathroom, holding on to steel bars used for support by ailing patients, and just as he had fixed himself in the middle of the swimming pool, he refused to move, from where he happened to plant himself, inviting force, his arms and legs black and blue and aching.

John was his only visitor. He tried, in vain, to persuade him to be more compliant and avoid being hurt. He was puzzled that a docile old man like Patryk could have the strength to hold on to bannisters and doors and refuse to be moved.

When John talked about the tragic incident, Akay had wondered what it was that made Patryk want to cling to things, to resist being moved from a position he had fixed himself, unaware of the absurdity of his bizarre behaviour. What sort of psychological condition would induce a normally docile man to resist any attempt to persuade him to return to his bed, to create in him a frenzied trauma, an inexplicable strength to resist the nurses and the security guards?

Now it was clear. The Gestapo had pulled him from his mother's arms and the violence imprinted itself on his brain. There could have been many more instances in his life when force had been used and when he felt he had to stay put, may be take a stand against danger, whatever this perceived danger might have been.

***

Akay wished that the little man would talk more but could see that this was not possible. John, concerned for Patryk, started gesturing again that questioning should end. Akay felt he'd gone too far and attempted to move the conversation on to a different topic.

'So how did you end up in England then?' he asked, hoping that the memories would be happier.

'I am not sure,' said Patryk. 'Our mother's doing, I guess.

She knew powerful people or maybe, worked at the British Embassy before it was called back to England and must have pleaded with the ambassador for help. I don't know really,' he said. He seemed troubled but soon calmed down.

'*An ambassador in Poland in the middle of World War Two was an unlikely assumption*,' thought Akay, but did not interrupt.

'We were put on a boat destined for England and ended up in a boarding school. It was good at first. We had food and were warm. My brother did well, went to university and set up an accountancy business. My experience was ok. As you know, there is a lot that goes on in boarding schools and I fell victim once my brother left the school for university. In time, I guess I learnt to enjoy being subservient.'

A smile, almost mischievous, broke out on his face and he was silent for a bit before continuing, 'Anyway, It's all in the past,' he concluded.

Once more, he focused on his gammon and chips. He was eating faster now, keen to clean up his plate, perhaps for fear that it would be taken away from him.

Akay's order had still not arrived. 'Soon be here, sir,' the waiter had said and disappeared. He asked John not to wait as his fish and chips would get cold. He then brought out his mobile phone. He tapped on google, typed in Krakow-Plaszov and pressed enter. A string of writing began to appear on the screen. He focused on the first paragraph:

'The Płaszów or Kraków-Płaszów was a German labour and concentration camp built by the Nazis. The Płaszów camp, originally intended as a forced labour camp, was constructed on the grounds of two former Jewish cemeteries in the summer of 1942 during the Nazi German occupation of Poland. In 1943, the camp was extended and subsequently became a concentration camp with deportations of the Jews from the Kraków Ghetto beginning October 28, 1942. Commanding the camp was Amon Göth, an SS commandant from Vienna who was known for being uncommonly sadistic in his treatment and killings of prisoners. On March 13, 1943, Göth personally oversaw the liquidation of the Kraków Ghetto, forcing its Jewish inhabitants deemed capable of work into the camp. Those who were declared unfit for work were killed. Under him were his staff of Ukrainian SS personnel, followed by 600 Germans of the SS-Totenkopfverbände (1943-1944), and a few SS women, including Gertrud Heise, Luise Danz, Alice Orlowski and Anna Gerwing.'

So that's where he was, a child and his older brother, from a mixed marriage, was sent to the concentration camp because they were not Arians. 'It all makes sense now,' thought Akay, and decided not to probe any further. His steak and ale pie had arrived. For a while, they ate in silence. Akay poked at his pie and ale ate a little. It had dried up. '*It must have been frozen and was defrosted in the microwave for too long, perhaps forgotten in there,*' he thought and pushed the plate aside.

Presently, Patryk spoke again, 'Our mother came to England too. Or maybe she was already here... I am not sure. But for some reason, we never lived with her. We were able to visit from time to time when she sent for us. We stayed as boarders until adulthood and then we didn't really want to live with her. She died a while ago.'

When my brother got married, I felt I should move out of his house. I felt it best that I should. We are still close. He does my accounts; he got me the flat I live in now. I could not have done it on my own. Nijela, my sister in law is nice too. They never had any children for some reason. Strange that, isn't it?' he said, and again a smile lit his face.

Once more, silence ensued and stayed with them all the way back to Chingford Mount. Outside, the expanse was suddenly busier with dog walkers. Groups of schoolchildren had stepped out of Queen Elizabeth's Lodge, now a museum with sixteenth century relics, and were hanging around the gardens, being blown about by the cold wind from the lush green expanse below the historic building.

Driving back through the high street was slow. Normally a quiet shopping area on the outskirts of London, bordered by Epping Forest, it too, was busy. Younger children were collected from the private school by parents in huge, fashionable four-wheel drive cars in contrast to carers on foot, often escorting two or three children, from the local state schools, alongside theirs, some in school uniform, others in pushchairs or prams. They soldiered through the crowd towards their home to consume afternoon tea cakes bought from the co-op supermarket, and drink water from multi-coloured beakers.

Older children were hanging around the Kentucky Chicken take away place. A few were waiting their turn for a haircut in the only barbershop in which, unusually, Eastern European young women worked as barbers and tried to communicate with customers in broken English. High pitched utterings replaced the words they did not know and they swayed back and forth in agreement with what the punters were saying but in truth, not getting the gist.

The Ridgeway was still quiet. At Chingford Mount, they descended the steep hill and met with more traffic. Inching their way along the main road, Akay commented on the much-changed town centre. There was a sprinkling of restaurants offering 'Ethnic food' on each side of the high street. Some shops had closed, but new ones had sprung up. A Turkish supermarket and a sizable eatery serving kebabs had replaced what was once a pub. He marvelled at the vibrancy of once a dull shopping area and thought foreign cuisine, must have breathed new life into it.

Soon through the traffic lights at the crossroads, they began to move faster. Within minutes, they reached the sheltered housing complex where Patryk lived, a red brick three-storey building with communal sitting areas. He stepped out of the old car.

'Back to my lonely abode,' he murmured under his breath. Then, turning to Akay, he said, 'Thank you, young man, I enjoyed that!' He hobbled into the building through the green door and disappeared. Halfway up the stairs, he emerged again. He stood on the half-way landing, shielded with glass to let in light and waved for a while before taking the next flight of stairs up to his apartment on the first floor. He didn't think of taking the lift-up.

'Funny little man,' said John. 'I never knew that. Do you know, he has thousands of pounds in the bank but won't spend any of it? There is hardly anything in his fridge, and sometimes, when we decide to meet on the weekend, he orders the cheapest item on the menu and digs deep into his pocket to find enough to pay for it. Sometimes, he brings a lot of change which annoys the cashier at the pub. I think he tries to live on the state pension which doesn't go far these days. With that sort of money in the bank, he can't claim benefits, so he chooses to live like a pauper. I wouldn't mind, but he has no one to leave it to. The taxmen will get it all.'

'*That too, makes sense,*' thought Akay, remembering Patryk's comment about being hungry at the concentration camp. He started reversing the car to deliver John to his house. At the entrance, John stood and waved for a while. It was his turn to make peace with loneliness. Soon, he too, would be moving into a retirement home.

'*A strange arrangement,*' thought Akay on his way back. A block of flats that houses a community of elderly people with a concierge who ensures that the building is safe as best she or he, can, and rings each resident, every morning, to check if they are ok. If they had fallen earlier in the morning, they would have to wait for her call between ten and eleven before they could get help. If they happen to fall on the weekend, or have a stroke, the waiting would be longer, their chances of survival, much reduced. True, there was a care line they could pull and call for help, but this was conditional on being able to get to the alarm string that hangs from the ceiling down to the floor.

'*Who could have invented such a set up,*' he thought, shaking his head. '*Such was the state of a caring system, a welfare state starved of cash and morally bankrupt. I hope I never need to move into such a place,*' he thought. And yet, they were comfortable flats. Far better than being abandoned or having to sleep out in the open. He remembered reading about the Chinese elderly who left their homes voluntarily to die of exposure. They left so that their young could share the food they themselves would have consumed, had they stayed.

Ironically, Patryk had money, and the supermarkets had plenty on their shelves. He had saved for a rainy day. The rainy day was here, but he wouldn't use his savings. He wasn't even aware that the rainy days had arrived. He was in a world of his lonely self, thinking lonely thoughts, waiting to die.

Akay took comfort from the fact that John would resist, would put up a staunch fight before giving up, giving in. 'Good for him,' he said, feeling more cheerful as he drove back to some household chores. His wife was still working. There wasn't much to do. He had prepared the ingredients for the evening meal earlier in the day. 'I'll put it in the oven half an hour before Sonay arrives,' he told himself before he went out to lunch. He cleared the sink and put the food in the oven on a low heat. He then went into the living room and sat gazing at the normally lush green garden now lifeless with the fall of winter.

In a while, he was asleep and was dreaming: It was a warm day and the sun shone brilliantly. His mother Emine, lay on the cool ground, under the bitter-orange tree, in the courtyard of the cottage she was allocated when she crossed the border into North Cyprus. She was dressed in white. She had had a stroke and lay in bed paralysed; unable to speak for over two years. Her right leg which gangrened was amputated a month before she died but it was now intact.

'Mother! How are you?' asked Akay.

'Eh so and so,' she answered.

'Those two years, were they difficult?'

"Difficult' is a euphemism,' she said, smiling.

'And now? How are you now?'

'As you can see,' she said.

'She looks calm, almost serene. And she can talk,' he murmured in his dream.

Just then, his wife, Sonay, came in, served herself some food which was on the verge of being burnt. She took a portion on a plate, brought it into the living room, sat in the coach opposite Akay and began to eat. Akay did not want to come out of the dream. He'd hoped his mother would appear in his dream one day, and she had. He was awake now. He opened his left eye first and then the right. He was still smiling.

'*Hayırdir*, auspicious dream?' enunciated Sonay, curiously.

'I don't know. I can't remember my dreams,' murmured Akay and tried to go back to sleep, to dream more. Alas, Emine was gone. She came to say she was well. Never again would she visit!

Kâzım Altan
24.08.2020